a justified hall pass

DENISE ESSEX

contents

I dedicate this book to any woman who needs assurance that her real life happily ever after is on the way!

acknowledgments

I'd like to acknowledge:

My family: Thank you for allowing me to take up space as an author.

My Marketing Director: You the real MVP! Thank you for believing in me and pushing me to be my best.

Latisha and proofreaders: Thank you for your patience with my commas and all the invaluable information you share!

My accountability partners: Thank you for motivating me with your inspiring goals and holding space for mine!

Me: Thank you for *continuing* to do it, despite your fears. I see you, Goddess!

Readers: Thank you for taking time from your life to play in my world and support my art!

dear reader,

Thank you for your interest in *A Justified Hall Pass*. Please **leave a five-star rating and review on Amazon and tag me on TikTok**. Also, be sure to recommend it to your friends. **Follow me on Amazon**, and sign up for my mailing and SMS list so we can keep in touch.

One of the best ways to support me as an indie author is to purchase a paperback. Find them on <u>Amazon,</u> or for a signed copy, visit my Etsy store.

Mailing list

    Get steamy texts from your favorite book baes 💋

    With love,

    Denise Essex

one

Bree

"FOURTEEN MONTHS!"

"Keep your voice down," I begged. Although most of the other Melanin Majesty Marketing employees had cleared out for the evening, I still didn't want her to tell my business to the world.

"No. You've gone fourteen months without sex! That fucking Lance. This has to be spousal abuse," Chanté added for good measure.

"I would say more neglect than abuse."

Walter had rounded the corner and entered my office. He dropped the file of the company we'd spent the last two weeks tirelessly prepping for, onto my desk. Walter, who most people referred to as Walt, had been one of my best friends since undergraduate school. He was a grumpy loner with a good heart. Although he had emotional quills like a porcupine, I saw him for who he truly was.

He was older than me and the other students in college because he started at the age of twenty-two. Instead of going straight to college after being homeschooled, he learned a trade and worked for four years. I was so enamored with the unique way he saw the world that his rough edges didn't bother me—we'd been friends ever since—and four years ago, Chanté joined my best friend's crew.

At Melanin Majesty Marketing, M3, we provided consumer reports and feedback to corporations to increase their sales. From Walter and my research alone, our last corporation would increase sales by millions. Walter and I started at M3 around the same time. He and I were already close because we'd practically grown up together. Now we were part of the handful of minorities on the team. It was a heavy weight to bear, to be both excluded and desperately needed.

For the past few years, Walter and I received emails from colleagues and team leads, asking if a particular advertisement would get them sued for racially discriminatory undertones. Walter was the first to demand that the two of us receive compensation for halting our workload to address aspects of contracts we weren't assigned.

My skin flushed at his declaration of Lance's behavior as neglect.

"Bree, girl, I'm sorry. I didn't know your fine ass work husband was here."

I hated when she did that. She and Walter were my best friends. He was a breath of fresh air in a workplace where I was often overwhelmed. I had a husband. Even though it had been over a year since we slept together, it didn't change my vows.

"Hey, Chanté. It's always a pleasure to see you." Walter pulled her in for a warm embrace. He gave the best hugs. His tight grip melted the stress away like no other hug I'd ever experienced.

"Don't flirt with me, boy. I'm not a saint like this one," she added, flustered from his strong arms.

"How's Chase?"

She rolled her eyes upward as she slipped out of his hold. "Why you gotta bring up my damn husband?"

Walter lifted his shoulders and flashed her a mischievous smile. "I like him."

"Ugh. I need to go get dinner ready." Chanté hugged me and threw her hand in Walter's face when he went for another one. "No, thank you. I can't even fantasize in peace, thanks to your mention of my man."

I loved that crazy girl. She and Chase had been married for ten years. He was perfect for her. He let her run her mouth, but behind closed doors, she was a devoted and surprisingly submissive wife. Chase was nothing like Lance. He expressed his love to his wife in ways *she* could understand. I wanted to keep faith that Lance loved me, but as the months rolled by, it got harder and harder.

I waved goodbye as she left me alone with Walt's curious eyes fixed on my profile.

"About that—"

"You don't owe me an explanation." He took a seat across from my desk and stretched out his long legs. Walter was comfortable in my space because we spent most of our time at work in each other's offices. We rarely spoke about Lance though. Walter didn't approve of him any more than Chanté.

Walter's breaking point was when we had an overnight work trip, an hour away from our small town, and I got sick with a terrible flu. The concern on Walt's face when he came to my hotel room let me know it was more serious than a cold. He found my phone and called Lance, who couldn't be bothered. When Walter drove me home, we bumbled through the front door to find Lance engulfed in a movie he didn't have the good sense to pause. I'd never forget how Walter's fist and jaw clenched.

Now, my best friend lightened at the mention of Lance's name. I could only imagine what he thought.

"Ask for a hall pass."

"A what?" I heard what he said, but I was a good girl. A good *Christian* girl. There was no way I'd agree to cheating on my husband.

"You heard me—a hall pass... to take care of your... neglect."

My cheeks were brown, but I was sure they tinted at his suggestion.

"Lance doesn't strike me as the kind of man who would mind."

I crossed my arms. "How so?"

Walter had a habit of touching his top lip to his nose when he wanted to choose his words carefully with me. It was thoughtful, but it still bugged the crap out of me.

"If you were my wife, not that I believe in marriage, you wouldn't need to ask. I'd please you regularly."

I had no doubt the women Walter dealt with were thoroughly satisfied. It was the unhurried way he walked and how he stared at the object of his desire as if they were the only person on earth. He was easy on the eyes too. I was married but not blind. When we met, he had starter locs that stood atop his head.

Now they hung down past his wide shoulders. To be out in public with him was uncomfortable, to say the least. Women couldn't tell whether we were a couple or related. No one ever accepted the two of us were strictly friends.

I wished Walt could be close with Lance like he was with me. Maybe he could influence my husband in the ways of wooing a woman. I was hopeful but confident that would never happen.

"Why wouldn't he question why I'd discovered you had the flu the time I brought you home?"

"Lance knows we're friends."

"Yeah, OK. Let my girl have a male friend bring her home. I'm a wonder where her female work friends are."

"It would be different if our friendship was new. I've known you for close to fifteen years. Besides, you're not jealous of men around Melina like that."

Melina was Walter's current situationship. She was a beautiful, talented woman who he would only continue to entertain if she didn't pressure him into a commitment. From what I could tell, she already wanted more than he was willing to give.

"That's not the point. Trust me, Lance won't bat an eye about giving you permission to have a weekend of consequence-free pleasure without him."

Walter wasn't joking. A hall pass was something white folks did on television, and it would still be an affair, with or without Lance's consent. My loyalty wouldn't allow me to do anything that wild.

"This is insane."

"Is it?"

Walt was always up for a debate. It was the reason he and I were such a great team. I would suggest a company take a specific approach to reach their target audience, but he'd lay out exactly why it wouldn't translate to a successful ad campaign. Most times he provided an alternative solution, so I let his argumentative nature slide.

"Yes, and it's cheating."

Walter stood and stretched. "Just think about it. You're one of the dopest people I know. There's no way you shouldn't be having good sex."

He stepped around my desk and pulled me into a similar embrace to the one he gave Chanté. "See you on Monday, Bree Bree."

"Bye, Walter."

When he was in the doorframe, he reiterated, "Get a hall pass, Bree. You deserve it."

Walter

HOW THE FUCK had Lance gotten so got damn lucky. Brielle Kari Thomas, formerly Brielle Barnes, was a saint. As far as I was concerned, she walked on water. No matter how big or small the task, Bree pitched in to help her coworkers, family, and friends.

Lance and Bree had a toddler together. He was a beautiful kid, despite his strong resemblance to his father. Her son had to be the reason she stuck around, because even the vows had to disagree with Lance's bullshit.

Bree operated like a single mother, and it irritated the shit out of me. She *wasn't* a single mom. She had a fully grown husband who made little effort to pitch in. I knew what Bree made in terms of salary because we worked at M3 for the same length of time. Lance was between jobs. I didn't judge him for it. I'd been there myself.

But Bree told me she did the cooking, she shuttled her son to daycare, and now I heard he wasn't fucking her. *That muthafucka is gay!* There was no other explanation. Bree was thick and possibly not everyone's cup of tea, but she was also undeniably fine. It took everything in me not to stomp his ass when she had the flu. She told me the following week, when she came back to work, she had to beg him to bring her soup.

If anybody deserved a hall pass, it was Bree. She'd been my friend for years, and I wanted nothing but the best for her. With only my newly pressed thoughts in my head, I imagined how this sneaky link might play out.

What if she chose a psycho stalker? I could make sure he was up to her standards. I knew Brielle better than she knew herself. I would be patient with her as she learned how to receive for once. Between Chanté and I, we would make sure Bree had the best weekend of her life.

Bree

I THOUGHT about Walt's dumb idea for a hall pass all weekend. What kind of loose woman would I have to be to agree to that? I didn't know why I let him get under my skin. Just because he could do whatever he wanted didn't mean I was afforded the same luxury.

Walter and I ended up at a company centered around beauty products for black women, but in a specialty for the organization where we were in the minority. Our friendship blossomed during that time, because Walter saw me at my worst and still hadn't judged me for it.

I sat with London in my lap as I visualized the demands of the coming week. London was Lance's and my rambunctious eighteen-month-old. He had the ability to transmute my stress into pure love. London only said a dozen words, but we still had full-blown conversations. Drool dripped from his face as he clapped a colorful toy in his hand and repeated the word 'ball' again and again.

After lunch, I laid London down for his nap and slipped into a nightie I purchased on the way home from the office Friday night. Lance got home late, and I'd fallen asleep by the time he'd arrived. It was Sunday afternoon now. I was rested, and London was fast asleep. I put on a pair of heels to make my intentions clear and sashayed down to Lance's man cave.

It was the top of the new year. My only resolution was to save my marriage and get laid by any means necessary. The fire-engine red nighty and matching red pumps accentuated my best features. I was five feet three, so I wore heels to add the illusion of height to my short yet thick frame.

Over the course of our three-year marriage, I'd come to doubt Lance's interest in me. We were both in our thirties and shouldn't be in a dry spell until much later. *Right?*

I tried to take my concerns to my mom, but she dismissed me, of course. She said there were men who went upside their women's heads and men who had outside children. My mother shamed me for complaining about not getting enough sex. I pushed those thoughts to the back of my mind. I was freshly showered and covered in the new scent I swiped from the mall.

Three black leather recliners sat across from the entertainment system. The recessed lighting added to the relaxed vibe that was fit for a king. I slowly shuffled down the steps, muting the clack of my heels so I wouldn't announce myself prematurely.

Lance was engulfed in a football game and didn't bother to lift his head in my direction when I entered the room. The fully remodeled basement was my birthday gift to him. He mentioned his need for space, and I did the heavy lifting to get a pool table and large screen television in the home without his knowledge. It was tricky because he didn't have a standard job like me. The night he first saw it, we made love most of the evening.

My body craved the level of passion we experienced last year on his birthday. Lance loved me in red, and he couldn't deny my swag when I wore heels.

"Hey, you," I said in a syrupy sweet tone.

"What's up?"

Be patient with him. You can do this. I coached myself through a conversation that would have left most women discouraged. Not me. Faith was ingrained in my DNA. From as far back as I could remember, I was taught that, with belief the size of a mustard seed, I could move mountains. Surely, I could entice a man like Lance to another night of unforgettable passion.

I sauntered to the center of the room in front of his eyeline. The TV was anchored to the wall above my head. I watched as the love of my life bounced his eyes enthusiastically between me and the game. I swallowed the lump in my throat.

There was no way I would show fear. A seductress took

rejection as a warmup to yes. I grew up in church, so I was well-versed in the Jezebel spirit. I'd seen evidence of its influence both growing up and out in the world. I could harness the same energy to keep my man's attention. God wanted marriages to work.

"The game is on, B," Lance said with his eyes still locked on the screen.

"I know, babe, but you can record it. London's down for a nap, and I thought maybe we could spend some *quality* time together." I stressed the word quality as I slowly walked in his direction. I maintained eye contact, although he... didn't. I climbed into his lap and straddled him.

When his hands gripped my waist, a wave of relief and excitement coursed through my veins. It had been too many nights without his touch. Finally, I would get the sexual healing I desperately needed. Before I could praise God, I was shifted off Lance's lap. He stood and rubbed his hand down his impeccable waves.

He didn't have a job, but he groomed himself like there was the possibility of an interview at any moment. There never was, and I didn't nag him about it. I was raised to work. Lance wasn't. But the least he could do was sleep with me. Was that too much to ask?

"I'm going to watch the game at *Grillin' and Chillin*," he announced.

Grillin' and Chillin' was a bar and grill restaurant where the men from the neighborhood gathered to escape the daily routines of their homes and enjoy food and football in peace. He leaned down and placed a quick peck on my lips, then bounded up the stairs and out of the house. A small tear wet my cheek as the front door closed and the hum of the garage rang out. I looked down at myself to make sure I was as sexy as I thought I was. *It's me. He doesn't want me.*

I was flustered when I arrived at work Monday morning. London spilled milk on my blouse just as we walked through the doors of the daycare. I considered asking Lance to meet me at work with a new shirt but immediately decided against it. We hadn't spoken since he ran out on me. When he finally got home last night, he took his dinner down to his man cave, while London and I watched his favorite cartoon.

Lance still slept in our bed, but most nights, he waited until I was asleep to join me. He hadn't done me any favors with that one. If I didn't get sex, the least he could do was hold me. He wouldn't.

I was at my breaking point. Something had to give. Still, I doubted I would muster up the courage to address it. I'd gotten to work five minutes early, but I was so frazzled from rushing around, it didn't matter.

"Happy Moonday, Bree Bree," Walter sang, his deep voice mocking me.

I liked to celebrate any occasion, including the start of the week. I regularly wished my coworkers a Happy Humpday and a Happy Friyay. He, on the other hand, couldn't care less.

"Don't start."

Walt rested a hand on his chest delicately with a gasp. "Oh my."

He stepped into my glass encased office and parked himself in one of the plush chairs that faced my mahogany desk. "For real, you good? Everything good with London Bridges this morning?"

My heart leaped. I had a soft spot for anyone who loved my son, and I took any opportunity to talk about how cute he was or what new thing he did. My entire demeanor softened. I plopped down with stars in my eyes.

"This morning when I parked the car at his daycare, I prepared for our normal prayer."

I saw Walter's eyebrows lift. He didn't participate in organized religion.

"I said, 'OK, bud, let's pray,' and he said, 'pwayyyy'."

Walter's lips curled into a pleased smile.

"Isn't he the cutest?" I aimed my phone in his direction to show him a picture of London with his pudgy hands somewhat clasped together.

"He looks like Lance, but he pulls it off," he admitted. "I don't really get the fuss about babies, but yours is cute."

"Thanks. It means a lot coming from Mr. Walter Simmons, the forever bachelor who doesn't do commitment or religion."

"I could do commitment, but I see no point in marriage."

I blew out a breath. "I'm in a good mood again. Please don't ruin it."

Walt shrugged his shoulders. "You're a wife. Give me one good reason why anyone should ever get married?" he challenged.

I swung my head to one side and crossed my arms. Why did he have to ask me this today? Normally, I'd have several reasons on deck. Suddenly, all my motivations eluded me.

"Well..." I hesitated. "Marriage is a blessing from God. It makes life fuller and richer."

Walt leaned forward in the chair and placed his elbows on his knees. "Is your life fuller, Brielle?"

I didn't like the soft tone he used with me. This wasn't counseling. Walt and I were friends long before I met Lance, and I had to admit the unwavering light I had years ago had dimmed.

I opened my mouth to respond but was interrupted by Aiden's shrill voice. *Thank God. I really don't want to lie.*

"Hey, you two. Joi wants everyone in the conference room in ten. Cool shirt, Brielle."

I gave him a forced smile. This was the shirt I almost broke my neck to get changed into before hustling clear back across town for work. Lance was still in bed. Aiden had unknowingly reminded me of the exact person I wanted to forget. I loved my husband, but I was sick of how awful his behavior had been, because he didn't try.

If he would just talk to me.

Walt towered over my desk with his long fingers in my face.

"Snap out of it. Where are you, Barnes?"

"My name is Bree Thomas."

"Your name is Brielle Kari Barnes." He smirked down at me, using my maiden name.

No matter how agitated I was with Walt, I had to admit he put me in a better mood.

"Whatever. Let's go."

Walt

I LOVED WHEN BREE SMILED. Her funky mood had something to do with her man. She didn't have to say it. They'd only been married a few years. At first, she insisted she'd found her better half, and all the other rhetoric that lovesick people said to justify irrational behavior. Out of my love for her, I gave buddy the benefit of the doubt.

But now, it was like the real Brielle was on the brink of fading to the background. In school, she rarely dated, so when she introduced me to Lance, I was stunned. He said all the right things, but if I was honest, I didn't trust his shifty ass eyes from the beginning. I could never figure out what the muthafucker did for work. He was like Tommy from *Martin*.

Everyone gathered into the conference room to prepare for an unscheduled meeting with Joi Cunningham. She was a driven sistah who had prioritized success over family. Now that she was in her early forties, her desire for a husband and child seeped from her pores. Bree and I had been with M3 for almost ten years. Joi was brought in less than a year ago when our former lead was caught up in a scandal with an administrative assistant.

The tall ceiling-to-floor windows provided natural light throughout the open space. I didn't mind these unnecessary exchanges, that could easily be emails, because the aesthetic was so calming. The bright sun was deceptive as the cool January temperature in McHaven was currently unforgiving. Fifteen identical, stylish chairs faced each other, while Joi stood facing us.

I swallowed hard as her eyes escorted my frame to my chair. Couldn't anybody else see the inappropriate way she stared at me? I hoped like hell I wouldn't have to talk to human resources. Joi was fine, but she wasn't my type.

"Your girlfriend likes you in charcoal slacks," Bree said as she leaned in and whispered beside my ear. I kicked her chair. The wheels made her collide with the back of Aiden's.

"Can you two lovebirds keep it down?"

Bree's light brown cheeks flushed. "Walt and I are—"

"Friends, we know." Aiden clapped hands with another one of our coworkers.

I didn't give a shit what they thought, but Bree did. After Aiden's comment, she kept her chair turned away from mine and positioned toward the front where Joi stood. As others from the team filtered in, my cell phone buzzed with a text from Melina. Melina and I had been together for three months. I didn't know what it was about women and the three-month mark, but her carefree facade had been replaced with an urgency to tie me down.

When I met her, she was uninhibited and disinterested in anything serious. I took her on dates where we sat down and had ample time to talk and get to know each other. At no point did she express interest in settling down. In fact, she insisted she wanted nothing more than a good time. This weekend, she asked what I thought about cohabitation. It hadn't been her first time skating around this subject.

I told her it was a fiscally responsible practice, although I had no desire in living with someone. Her hint was about the two of us. Melina wanted to move in without having to ask directly. She hoped she would be invited. After my response, she got up, dressed, then stormed out of my place.

She was thirty years old. Nothing turned me off faster than an immature woman.

MELINA:

Sorry about this weekend

ME:

For what?

I was too old for games. If she was going to apologize, she needed to use her words.

MELINA:

eye roll emoji For leaving the way I did Saturday

ME:

I accept

MELINA:

What do you have planned for Thursday?

Shit! I told her about my birthday once. Apparently, she remembered. What slipped her mind was that I didn't celebrate my birthday. There was no point in making a big fuss about what was truly my mother's commemorative day. I didn't birth me.

"Now that the team is here, let's get started," Joi announced.

ME:

I'm in a meeting. I'll talk to you later

I lifted my head to see Bree with a smirk on her face. Her nosy ass stayed in my business.

"She's getting too close," she whispered but turned her chair before I could respond.

While Melina didn't much care for my friendship with Bree, Bree had her back. She often took Melina's side in our spats. Bree's goody two shoes demeanor and Christian beliefs would never allow her to shack up, but she said it wasn't unreasonable for Melina to express interest.

"This project is all hands on deck. Brielle and Walter have a fabulous track record with our client, *CocoaKiss Cosmetics*, but this time, they've partnered with a celebrity."

I gritted my teeth. This celebrity was likely an untalented, social media curated persona who would inevitably impede my ability to advertise.

"You know what that means. They will mistake the size of their platform as experience in the art of advertisement. That's why we need to sit down with our client and the talent in person. We'll be doing just that a month from now in Florida."

Bree stiffened. A flight to Florida was several hours away from where we lived and worked. Unless she got her mom or one of her brothers to fly with her, she'd have to leave London Bridges at home for days. She hated to be away from him for more than two nights.

"I know everyone has a life, but this trip is non-negotiable. You're expected to be in Florida for four days minimum. At least half of the team needs to be available the entire week. Those of you who can't bear to be away for the duration must commit to being on call for the remaining three days. You can attend the less essential meetings remotely."

Aiden raised his hand, which earned him a scowl from Joi.

"Yes, Aiden."

"Who's the talent?"

Aiden was a textbook know-it-all. He rubbed people the wrong way, yet he had no clue why. I was homeschooled and had my own loner issues, but I wouldn't be surprised if Aiden didn't have some sort of undiagnosed social disorder. The reality was, we all wanted to know the same thing; we just had the good sense not to ask.

"Great question. I don't need to remind you that you signed confidentiality agreements during your on-boarding."

Several team members whispered about who it was. Some laughed at her reminder to keep the information to ourselves. It meant we would work with an A lister.

"And, if this collaboration is leaked, it could ruin bonuses for everyone," Joi insisted.

"Just keep your mouth shut online and in your family group chat with your nana who gossips like it's her profession," I added.

The water in Bree's mouth sprayed, and a couple others joined her in laughter.

"Thank you, Walter." Joi's gaze lingered in my direction.

I wasn't interested in her, but I'd use my charm to get the information I wanted. "No problem. We'll be on our best behavior. You can tell us." I didn't break eye contact, but she did.

With her head lowered and a smirk on her face, she huffed. "The new lip care line will be released by Zanaé."

"Damn."

Bree turned around and slapped my leg. I'd had the biggest crush on Zanaé since she came out. For the most part, I stayed on my best behavior. I was something like a gentleman, but Zanaé was fine for no reason. I had no problem expressing my thoughts about exactly what I wanted to do to her.

There was something about a small woman with a monstrous personality that sent chills up my spine. Generally, I was an ass man, but for Zanaé, I would make an exception. Unfortunately for Brielle, she had to hear all about it.

"I'm going to be pissed if Walter gets one on one time with her," Aiden muttered.

"Aht aht," Bree chimed in. "Don't be a hater."

Aiden pursed his lips. Why the hell was he so invested? He swore Bree and I were together one minute. He tried but failed miserably to shoot his shot with Melina. Now he was salty at the mere thought that I could get semi-alone time with Zanaé.

"Don't worry, Aiden. I'll get a picture for you."

"There will be more details later in the week." Joi gathered her belongings and left the conference room.

Bree stood and slowly placed a pen and notebook into her designer bag. She refused to take digital notes because she was adamant that she retained information better when she wrote longhand. She said nothing as the others emptied the room, invigorated by the coming collaboration.

I fell in step with her as she moseyed toward her office.

"You give any more thought to the hall pass?"

Her slanted eyes found mine.

"Huh?"

"The trip would be a great time."

She blinked up at me.

"Have you thought about it?" I pressed.

"No," she lied. Bree was a bad liar. It was cute.

"Yeah, you have."

She stumbled into her office, and I held in my laughter. In all the years that I'd known her, Bree was still uncomfortable with conversations about sex.

"I'm not cheating on my husband, Walt."

I gazed down at her. I was prepared for a sermon, or even a sassy retort, but the defeated expression that draped her chestnut features shook me to the core. Bree deserved to be cherished. She was owed sexual satisfaction of the highest degree, and if Lance wouldn't give it to her, it was her right to find it elsewhere.

"I hear you. I'm gonna shut my mouth about it."

"But?" A slight smirk spread across her lips, and it warmed my heart. These days, she was so sensitive I feared I pushed too hard. She was different from when we first met. I was the same.

"But... consider the difference between cheating and getting your needs met for once."

She crossed her arms.

"I mean, if you have needs. Maybe you don't have sexual needs. Some of y'all women be like camels."

"What?"

"You know, able to have sex once then go long spells without it."

She flung a hot pink stack of Post-its at my head, but I caught them.

"I can barely go more than a week," I muttered.

"Goodbye, Walter."

She dismissed me. It wasn't the first time, and it wouldn't be the last. Bree deserved to get her back broken from unadulterated, uninhibited sex more than most. If Lance wouldn't do it, she should use her hall pass in Florida. I could keep an eye on her and make sure nobody took advantage. It was a win-win. I just had to get Brielle on board.

two

Bree

LONDON HAD A FEVER FOR TWO NIGHTS IN A ROW. I TOLD
my coworkers I would be home but available virtually for meetings.
When I took him to the pediatrician, they said he had a double ear
infection. My poor baby had an ear infection before, but this was
the first time they threatened to put tubes in his ear if he got
another one. All I heard was surgery. I lost it.

My eyes filled with tears, and I was sure the nurses were
seconds from placing a call to protective services for my exaggerated
response. I wasn't only upset about the mention of the procedure; I
was pissed that I had to process this information on my own. Lance
refused to come because he said there was no need for both of us to
be at appointments. I would go no matter what, but I still wanted
support.

Lance was a better father than he was a husband, but like most
dads, he was too laid back for my liking. He never asked the doctors
questions, and he rarely told me what was discussed on the rare

occasions I couldn't get away from work. He was of the mind that I should trust he had it handled. He wasn't completely wrong, but neither was I.

I fought the urge to call him while I awaited the prescription for antibiotics. An exchange with Lance while I was emotional would be like a trip to the hardware store for milk—I wouldn't get the reassurance I desired. With the script in my hand and London fast asleep in his car seat, I dialed Chanté.

"How's my nephew?"

I loved that I didn't have to explain myself with my girl. We spoke last night, and I told her if London's fever didn't break, I would take him to get looked at. The sob I buried while I was in the pediatrician's office bubbled to the surface.

"Bree, what happened?"

"I know it's silly, but they said if he has another one, he'll need surgery."

Chanté took a deep breath. "Where are you? Are you home?" There wasn't a hint of judgment in her tone.

"Not yet. We're in the parking lot of the pediatrician."

I sniffed. To be seen was a luxury I wasn't accustomed to. It was the reason I clung to my friendships with Chanté and Walt. Walt made fun of me and didn't agree with my lifestyle choices, but he respected me. They both saw me. On the other hand, my family didn't take the time, and Lance couldn't be bothered.

"Big breath, baby."

I did as she instructed and lifted my shoulders to relax.

"Are you OK to drive?"

I nodded my head and chuckled to myself because she couldn't see me. "I am. This is Walt. I'll call you when I get home."

"Hey," I said when I hung up with Chanté to accept his call. I prayed he couldn't hear the remnants of sadness in my voice. The last thing I wanted was a lecture or questions about why I chose to live like a single mother. It wasn't my choice.

"What's wrong with you, Bree Bree? Your man fuckin' up?"

"I have you on speaker phone, fool."

"My bad, London Bridges. Yo' daddy actin' up?"

"He's asleep. Thank God."

"Talk to me, girl."

I put the car into drive, confident I could make it home safely, thanks to my best friends. I filled him in then told him I would speak to him once I got London settled. How could I be wildly successful in work and friendship but an utter failure with my family and in my marriage?

The pediatrician was only twenty minutes from my house, and I was more peaceful than I'd been before I left. But my eyes welled with fresh tears when I saw Chanté's and Walt's cars parked in front of the house. *Did they coordinate this? And how the hell did they make it here so fast?*

I parked in the driveway and unloaded London and his diaper bag. I was excited to see my people, despite my fear about my baby's ear infections. They both stood by Chanté's car in a hushed conversation. When I walked up, she took London—who was ridiculously heavy these days. Walt grabbed everything else in my hands.

"Explain to me why his simple ass is cleaning your gutters while you're freaking out and home from work?"

"Who?" I figured Walt was referring to Lance, but when I looked around, he was nowhere in sight.

Chanté pursed her lips. "He's in the back. Barely spoke to us."

"He thinks y'all don't like him," I admitted.

"I can't speak for Chanté, but I sure as hell can't respect a man who has his wife out here living like a single mother. You do everything."

London, who shared the same face as Lance, continued to nap.

"Let's get my baby inside," Chanté cooed.

I had no doubt that if she didn't have him in her arms, she would have ripped Lance a new one, right along with Walter.

Once we were all settled in my house, I put London in his bed. I brought the baby monitor with me to the loft where the three of us sat.

"Why aren't y'all at work?" I asked. I was much more relaxed now that I was in their presence, but they had other obligations.

"You know I go to that plantation when I feel like it. Long as my work is quality and it gets done, they know better than to ask where I'm at," Walt volunteered. His long legs were stretched across the entire loveseat like he belonged in my home. It warmed my heart that my friends were comfortable here.

"I do good work too, friend. They only get mad that I'm gone when they need a blacksplanation. I'm the go-to for all things urban."

The three of us shook our heads at that one.

"Now let's get down to business. How is this hall pass gonna work?" Chanté asked. She looked to Walt for feedback.

"We got a work thing coming up in Florida. I say you meet her out there, and she should just do it then," Walt responded. They conversed like I wasn't in the room.

"Excuse me," I interjected.

"When is the Florida trip? I can put in a request for time off now. Chase and I need some adult time, if you know what I mean."

Walt bobbed his head knowingly. I didn't. In the beginning, Lance couldn't keep his hands off me. Once we had established routines, our sex tapered, but we never went more than a week and a half before we reconnected. After I had London, I did gain weight, but plenty of men loved my extra thickness.

I got hit on and approached incessantly during my pregnancy. I had a man offer to take care of me and the baby, because he swore I was that fine. However, Lance grew distant during that time. When I asked him about it, he said I was overly sensitive because of my hormones. Then he lost his job. He hadn't worked since I returned to M3 after my maternity leave.

My hairdresser told me to watch out. I'd been vocal about the change in his behavior because I trusted her with my business. She said she'd seen too many high-earning black women get taken advantage of by man diggers. I almost fired her as my hairdresser when she casually suggested I get a postnuptial agreement. At first, Lance stopped initiating sex with me. When he started declining my advances, I took her advice and made him sign a postnup.

Chanté typed on her smartphone.

"It's next month," Walt offered.

"Perfect. Gives me plenty of time to get someone lined up to keep Hakeem."

"I'm sitting right here," I said.

They had the nerve to make plans as if I would agree to something as treacherous as an affair. Lance wasn't in the running for husband of the year, but he didn't deserve to be cheated on because we were in a rough patch. All successful couples went through tough times. Even the FLOTUS admitted to a ten-year period of disdain toward Barack. I prayed our difficult chapter wouldn't last that long.

"Did I tell you how much I love his name? Hakeem is truly a powerful name. How's he doing?" Walt asked.

"Yeah, you told me. Chase couldn't stop talking about you after you said that. He never lets me forget, because I was adamantly against it. It's too black," Chanté mumbled.

Does she still feel this way?

Walter sat forward on the sofa. A debate was on the horizon. I cleared London's toys as Walter's jaw tightened.

"Girl, what?" he asked.

"You heard me. Don't act like you don't know how white folks treat us based on our names. If he was a Chase Junior or Carter like I wanted to name him, he wouldn't be in the situation he's in now."

"What happened?" I asked. I paused my busy work to give her my full attention.

"His teacher put him out of class last week."

"For what?" Walt and I asked simultaneously.

"She said he was disruptive."

"But Hakeem loves school. And who was outside with him? He's in the first grade," I pressed.

"Exactly. Chase and I met with his teacher first thing this morning. She said he finishes his work then disturbs others." Chanté's shoulders sagged.

"Then give him something to do," Walt barked.

Chanté held her hands up to stop him. "You sound like my mama. Chase asked if we could send extra work with him to complete once he's finished with the daily requirements, and his teacher was fine with that."

"Let me get this straight. You came up with the solution *and* you have to supply the materials? What exactly is she doing?" Walt blurted.

"I'm with Walt on this one, boo," I told Chanté.

"What other choice do I have?" Chanté asked.

"Homeschool that king."

I wasn't surprised Walter suggested Chanté and Chase homeschool their son. He'd been homeschooled. But Walt's mother, Grace Simmons, was a saint. She had patience that rivaled mine. London was my world, but I couldn't fathom my days filled as both his mother and teacher.

"We're not here to talk about me," she said to Walt. "We're here to plan this nasty sex you're about to have, friend," Chanté said, bringing the focus back to me and my parched state.

It was true. I was about ready to climb the walls I was so wound up. What I wouldn't give to have Lance interrupt my worrying about our son with a tight grip around my neck and sex on our counter. I stared off, feeling heated as I fantasized about how Lance would feel inside of me again.

The front door closed, which shook me from my trance and alerted me that Lance had finished outside.

"Y'all are here to check on me and London. What good will come of trying to ruin my marriage?" I whispered sternly.

If Lance got wind of our conversation, I could guarantee he'd punish me with silence for at least a week.

"God helps those who helps themselves," Chanté offered. She shrugged her shoulders. Little did she know, I hadn't stopped praying for God to intervene in my relationship. The only New Year's resolution I had was to finally allow for a mutually satisfying sexual relationship. I would do everything in my power to make space for it in my marriage.

"That's not in the bible," Walt said with his head buried in his smartphone.

Both Chanté and I glared at him. Walt was the least religious person I'd ever met.

He peered up to find our eyes on him. "What? I've read many sacred texts, including the bible, both objectively and soberly. It's the blind trust in a book most people never bother to read that I don't agree with."

"He's right."

Our heads flew to the stairs where Lance ascended them. In search of what, I had no idea.

"Cleanliness is next to godliness isn't in the bible either, but my mama stayed using it to keep me in line," Lance added.

I saw Chanté roll her eyes and Walt's jaw tighten again. Lance didn't notice, so he continued. "That's not to say that you can have a clear mind with a cluttered ass house, but don't quote it like it's biblical."

Walter opened his mouth, but it wouldn't be in support of anything Lance had to say, even if he was right.

"I'm going to warm up food. Do y'all want some?" I asked before Walt could speak.

I wouldn't let Walter give me a headache. God and the hope that Lance would come around were all that I had to console me most nights. He had Melina, and Chanté had Chase. Neither of them could relate to the depth of my pain. Lance was happy with me once. We would get back there. I was positive we would.

Walt

"WHY ARE YOU SO GRUMPY TODAY?" Bree asked.

She breezed into my office like she didn't have a care in the world. The light in her that I remembered from years ago was back. Maybe London Bridges was better, or maybe Lance finally came to his senses and tapped that ass.

"Why are you so... sunny today?"

She rolled her eyes and dropped a stack of magazines on my desk.

"Where did you even find these? Who sells magazines?"

"Does it matter?"

In the grand scheme of things, it didn't, but I sensed a good old-fashioned homework assignment on the horizon, and the thought of it made my eye twitch.

"If we study these, I bet we could avoid the need to reinvent the wheel. I guarantee there's an angle we could recycle and get the job done," Bree said with bright eyes.

Just as I thought, she wanted me to do homework.

I flipped through the magazines, impressed at how many of the ads were intended for black audiences. It was the exact energy we needed to sell Zanaé. Although I was hesitant to work with a celebrity, the reality was if we could sell her, we didn't need to sell the product. Once consumers bought into her, they'd buy whatever she attached her name to. We could also guarantee her team that if we approached this rollout correctly, Zanaé would see an immediate increase in her music streams.

It was a win-win situation for everyone, and if I got the opportunity to see her up close and breathe her air, I could die a happy man.

Bree's mouth hung wide open like it did when she was deep in thought. I balled up a scrap of paper and threw it at her. It didn't go in, but it hit her lip and broke her from her trance. She blew out a breath. I might have gotten under her skin, but I kept her from taking the job too seriously. We did good work, and as a team, we were unstoppable.

"Spit it out. What's that big brain of yours cooking up?"

"What if we have her in the studio? Maybe they could use a snippet of a new track she's working on, and before they give away too much of the song, Zanaé stops recording to apply the product. She can say, 'When I look great, I sound great'."

I stroked the hair on my chin. Advertising was my forte. "So, you're doing my job now?" I teased. Bree's suggestion was incredible. It explained the renewed light I saw across her doll-like features. Or maybe her airy demeanor was the reason she came up with the idea with little effort. She eagerly awaited my thoughts, and I wouldn't be me if I didn't make her sweat.

My face was scrunched when I asked, "The studio?" I gritted my teeth and stood. "It's too predictable. A singer in the booth?" I shook my head and stole a glance at Bree. Her smile faded, and the corners of my mouth lifted.

"You're playing with me!"

"Yup. Can't let you get a big head, Bree Bree." I turned to peer out of my window and added, "Instead of, 'when I look great, I sound great,' how about 'when I look sexy, I sound sexy'?"

Bree jumped up and squealed. She high fived me like we were in kindergarten. I closed the space between us and squeezed her side, because Bree was extremely ticklish. Her squeals and futile attempts to get away fueled my pursuit. Her light brown skin was flushed as she laughed uncontrollably. My door swung open, and Aiden peeked in.

"Hard at work?"

Bree wiggled out of my grasp and smoothed her clothes. "We just came up with the campaign for Zanaé."

"That's exactly what it looks like. What makes you so sure Joi will approve of it?"

Aiden was a stealthy hater. He didn't come right out with his criticism, but he had a way of spreading doubt and trying to plant seeds that made his colleagues second guess their genius. I worked with him long enough to know how he operated. It didn't faze me, but it often penetrated Bree's delicate disposition.

Her sensitivity was one of the most charming qualities about her, but it left her susceptible to assholes like Aiden who pretended to be helpful. I saw right through him.

"Did you finish Joi's hotel accommodations?" I asked. Aiden had some balls to question Bree in front of me when most times Joi used him as a glorified administrative assistant.

Aiden opened his mouth like he'd speak but thought better of it. He backed out of my office and closed the door behind him.

"You wrong for that," Bree said as she gathered the stack of magazines. They hadn't helped with the idea for the ad. It was all her. "But thank you, Walt."

"Anything for you, Bree Bree."

"Mama, where you at?" I asked from inside the heavy door of my mother's quaint home. She still lived in the house I grew up in, although she kept the appearance as clean as any other modern property in the neighborhood.

"I'm in here."

I smelled fresh bread in the oven. It was a miracle I wasn't overweight with the way this woman cooked.

"Hey, Mama."

My mother placed the perfectly prepared bread on top of the stove and removed her oven mitt. She saw the excitement in my eyes and rested her fists on her wide hips.

"What?" I asked with a wide smile.

"This is for company."

"I'm company, Mama," I pleaded. It was child abuse to withhold her homemade bread from me.

"Boy!" She laughed.

"What else you made?"

"The weather's been cool these days, so I made soup."

I rubbed my hands together. I had only planned to stop by and say hello, but now I would stay for dinner.

"I can't wait to go to Florida."

"For work?"

"Yes, ma'am," I said as I bopped into the nearest bathroom to wash my hands.

"How is Brielle?"

"She's OK. London Bridges keeps getting ear infections."

"Oh, no. Tell her to bring him to me. Lord knows I'm not going to waste my breath praying for grandkids of my own."

I walked back into the kitchen and shook my head. "I got a few more years before my swimmers give up."

A loud whack shook my backside when my mother slapped me with a hand towel.

"What I do?" I asked as I chuckled.

"Don't joke like that." She pursed her lips and continued with her task. "Speaking of families, Melina stopped by."

I almost choked on the orange juice I pulled from the refrigerator.

"That's what you get. You know better. Get a glass, Walter Simmons."

I cleared my throat and set the juice on the countertop beside me. "When?"

"Earlier today. Said she wanted to know if you always skipped birthday celebrations or if it was her you didn't want to celebrate with."

"She's way out of line, Mama."

"Is she?" My mother grabbed a glass and poured my drink. She gave me a knowing look and returned the juice to the fridge.

I downed the orange juice and paused before I said something disrespectful in front of the woman who gave me life. "I like Melina. I really do."

"You don't have to convince me," my mom said with hints of laughter in her voice.

I wanted things to go smoothly with Melina, because if they didn't, maybe *she* wasn't the problem. I'd found another amazing woman with a flaw I wasn't willing to overlook. "I told her I don't do birthdays."

"I'm sure you did. You also know she's not the type of woman who does nothing on a day she considers a big deal," my mom noted.

"Ain't that the epitome of selfishness? She wants to give me a gift because it makes *her* feel good... regardless of if it's what I want?"

My mother walked toward the chair where I'd taken a seat and laid a reassuring hand on my shoulder. "I raised you to take up as much space as you deserve and to be as free as possible, but I warned you that everyone else didn't come up like you. If you want to be in healthy relationships, you've got to meet people where they are."

My shoulders sagged. *Am I supposed to let this woman force me to make birthday plans and let it slide that she popped up at my mama's house behind my back to fact check me?*

"If not her, then who?" my mom asked. She kissed my forehead and returned her attention to the soup that made my mouth water. I would deal with Melina Steward later. Right now, my stomach was in my back. I was so hungry.

three

Bree

I COULDN'T WAIT TO GET HOME. I HATED WHEN MY mornings started the way they had these last few weeks. I usually didn't mind doing all the things. Now, Lance had gone too far. He wouldn't pitch in unless I nagged him. And no mother in their right mind wanted an unwilling father to handle a boisterous toddler.

Mornings with London had become a struggle. It was as though he sensed he was about to be dropped off, and he wasn't onboard with that plan. Once he was distracted, he loved it at school, but the transition was hell. When London tossed his cereal at me or rubbed a sticky hand across my silk blouse, that tense mood followed me the rest of the day.

I drove past London's daycare. I left the office an hour early this afternoon and decided I could pick him up after I changed out of my work clothes and caught my breath. He didn't need to be around my chaotic energy. Based on the pictures sent to my phone, he'd just done finger painting with a few other painfully beautiful children.

My mind was still flustered with the news that I would have to spend almost a week in Florida. Walt loved my idea to have Zanaé in the studio with the product, and if Joi approved it, he wanted me to be the one to present it to Zanaé's team. I was beyond nervous about facing someone that famous.

I dreaded the conversation with my mom about my work trip. She swore she was available whenever I needed help, but then she'd complain that London's food and diapers were expensive. It was her way of hinting I should pay her for any of his overnight stays, despite the fact that I sent him with more than enough food, diapers, and clothes to last several weeks. I prayed that there would be a time when I could give my family money without guilt. They guilted me, and I let them.

I abhorred work travel that took me away from London for more than two nights. The worst part was that those work destinations were typically to middle America. On the bright side, Florida could serve as a vacation of sorts. I hadn't been on a pleasure trip since before London was born. I'd lost some weight in the past six months. Maybe I could look at bathing suits outside of the maternity section.

Walter's suggestion to step out on Lance popped back into my head as it had since he'd offered it as a solution to my drought. He was my friend, but I wouldn't let him plant seeds that had the potential to ruin my marriage.

I parked my car on the street instead of in the garage since I had to run back out to get London from daycare. There was a chance that Lance would do it, but if my car was inside the garage, I wouldn't want to leave the house again until morning. The last thing I wanted after the day I just had was a fight at home. I punched the code into our front door, and immediately, the hair on the back of my neck stood up.

Is somebody in my house? Lance was gone unless he'd parked his car in the garage. Something wasn't right. I ran to the safe hidden under the kitchen sink and pulled out the loaded revolver. My hands shook, and I thanked God London wasn't with me. I'd taken the classes and was certified in how to properly operate a firearm, but I'd never had to use my training.

I crept to the basement door that led downstairs to Lance's man cave with my bag still thrown over my shoulder. The lights were off. I moved toward the primary bedroom where a voice spoke through the television. It wasn't a show though—it was live.

Our home was expensive. We lived in a gated community, and although we didn't have cash stashed out in the open, we had valuables in every room. Maybe the trespasser called for online help.

When I slinked up to the cracked door, Lance was laid across our bed with his boxers and pants at his ankles. *Why would he be...* I angled my head to peek further in the room where he watched a live stream. There was a naked white woman on the screen of our seventy-five-inch television. I kicked the door open with the revolver still in my hand.

For the past year, when Lance looked at me, all I saw was irritation in his eyes. Not this time. Alarm covered his handsome features. I went deaf. I couldn't hear a thing. His mouth moved, but there was no sound. I was out of my body, somehow peering down at myself.

How did I get here? Memories of our wedding day and the evening we brought home a two-day-old London flashed through my mind. *How had things been so good and gone to hell just as fast?* I returned to my body at the sound of two clicks. I'd cocked the gun.

The wench's voice was shrill on the screen. She hadn't bothered to cover herself. She was comfortable in the nude. No wonder Lance preferred her. She hadn't had any children. It was obvious from her flat stomach and perky breasts. Mine hung because I breastfed our son for God's sake.

When my eyes slid back to Lance, he'd stood and had the good sense to pull his pants up.

"Why is your ex-wife in the house with you, baby?"

Her thick accent made the lunch swirl in the pit of my stomach.

"Ex-wife?" I found my voice and spoke for the first time.

"I can explain," Lance tried.

My hand was steady. They no longer shook, and I was prepared to take Lance Thomas's soul from his despicable body.

"London," he said.

I froze. Who would take care of my son if I killed his father? The thought that Lance and this bimbo might raise my son while I served time behind bars was like a cold glass of water to the face. I gasped. And though I had no intention to hurt anyone, I aimed the gun at the ceiling and shot it as a warning.

"Get the fuck out of my house!"

Walt

I SAT at home in front of my computer screen. I had no idea how long I'd been in a zone, but this week's article was nearly complete. I was inspired by the conversation I had with Chanté at Brielle's house last week. She joined us for lunch sometimes since her job was in the same industrial complex as ours, but this time, we'd made a house visit when we got word London Bridges was sick.

The fact that Chanté's six-year-old son was asked to step out of class because he 'disrupted' other children when his work was complete was ludacris.

The title of the blog was, *"Do Black boys and girls belong in the school system?"* For me, the answer was simple. Hell no. I had personal experience with teachers like whoever was entrusted with Chanté and Chase's son, Hakeem. Instead of punishment, the kid should've been rewarded for his ability to fly through the work.

I blogged to vent my frustrations about the systems in our society, and more than one went viral. I wrote my work under the pseudonym, The Lone Wolf, Dizzy D. Some of my friends from college called me Walt Dizzy, and since I didn't want to receive a cease and desist from the billion-dollar media conglomerate, I settled on Dizzy D. Other than Bree and Chanté, I kept to myself, hence The Lone Wolf.

After a long day at work and several hundred calls and texts from Melina, the practice of putting my thoughts into words was a form of therapy for me. My mother received criticism for her choice to keep me out of school. My confusion was the motivation to do my own research. The school-to-prison pipeline was enough to keep me from my fear of missing out on traditional school milestones. I was the type of person who needed to know the why behind everything. With the way school was set up, I would have been called disruptive too.

I ended the blog with a few statistics about teachers' bias when it came to black male children. Most primary school teachers were white women. The dynamics between a growing black male child and a white woman, who demanded complete compliance in order to feel safe, was not only backwards, but it was also the origin of policing our youth.

My advice for those who might be in situations like Hakeem and Chanté was to find a local homeschool group. That way, if both parents worked full time, the load could be shared within a community of like-minded parents. As a last resort, I suggested parents find a reputable charter school with staff that shared the same ethnicity and culture as the child.

I closed my laptop and powered my phone back on, which I'd turned off because I wrote best without distractions.

MELINA:

Are you ignoring me?

MELINA:

Who gets upset over someone asking what
they want for their birthday?

MELINA:

Can we talk about this?

BREE BREE:

I caught Lance online cheating. I'm a
mess. London is with my mom and Chanté
is over here plotting his murder. I could
have killed him, but I didn't. Help!

The hell? I took a few gulps of the beer in my hand. Melina would have to wait. Bree needed me.

I WAS glad I didn't get a ticket on my way to Brielle's. I'd passed at least three McHaven police cars, but none of them batted an eye. If Bree didn't kill Lance, I could make it happen for her.

I parked behind Chase's car. He must have driven his wife. Chase didn't trust Lance's ass to do the right thing and, therefore, as a man, couldn't in good conscience send his wife to console her friend alone. Bree was emotional and possibly fed up for good this time. The door swung open before I could knock.

"Hey, Walt. Good to see you, man. We could use a little more testosterone up in here." Chase laughed, but his smile didn't reach his eyes.

He stepped aside so I could enter. "How long y'all been here? She OK?"

"About an hour. She's as good as can be expected. Her mom got London, so hopefully, she lets Chanté give her something to put her to sleep. Right now, she's refusing. Too hopped up on adrenaline."

My chest tightened when my eyes landed on my best friend. Bree's tight natural curls were disheveled, and she still had her work clothes on, despite the late hour. Bree deserved to be treated like a queen. She should have someone to look out for her like Chase did for Chanté. I had no faith in marriage, but I could discern a functional one from a dysfunctional one.

Brielle paced the floor while Chanté whispered to her. When her eyes found mine, she stopped. I nodded at Chanté, then pulled Bree in for a hug. She melted into me while the fabric of my shirt moistened from her tears.

"It's okay, Bree Bree. We got you. I got you."

Bree

CHANTÉ AND CHASE said goodbye and promised to be back whenever I needed them. I wouldn't hesitate to take them up on their offer, but it was a school night, and I wanted them home with Hakeem. I locked up and took a seat across from Walter. There was no judgment nor pity in his eyes, and I appreciated it with my entire being.

He didn't speak, just patted his lap with a lazy grin on his face. Walter wasn't a softy by any stretch of the imagination, but when I was down—which seemed to be a lot these days—he was available to release the tension of the day. I put my feet in his lap, like I'd done a thousand times before, and let him massage away my fears and worries about the future.

"How's Melina?" I asked, desperate to shift the focus from my mess of a life.

Walter stopped his heavenly assault briefly. When I wiggled my toes, he continued. "She went to my mom's house to ask if I didn't celebrate my birthday at all or if I simply didn't want to celebrate with her."

"Oh," I said.

"It's not just the birthday thing that's annoying, but she also keeps hinting that she wants to move in."

I cringed for him. Walter could be unagreeable, and although I understood Melina's desire to live together, sis had to know that wasn't the move.

"Walter, she's been around for months. It's not surprising that she would want to move in with you."

He pressed the pad of his thumb into my foot. I was in heaven despite the literal hell from my real life. Walter gave the best foot rubs and Chanté the best mani pedis. *Thank you, God, for my friends.*

"If you rub her feet like you're rubbing mine, she'd be a fool not to want to move in with you."

He chuckled lightly. "I ain't never rubbed Melina's feet. Hell naw! I shouldn't be rubbing yours." He swatted my feet from his lap and stood. "I spoil you enough as it is."

"Somebody has to," I muttered. My throat burned, and tears threatened to fall from my eyes. I held onto them for dear life. I couldn't handle yet another cry-induced migraine.

"Where's the shit Chanté left to put you to sleep?"

I pointed. Walter grabbed the pill and my sparkling water. "Here. Take this with your bourgeois ass water."

I smirked. Walter stayed with the jokes about how I drank European water for the snooty.

"And Lance is an idiot for not spoiling you the way you deserve. I should kick his ass."

Once I took the medicine, I lay across the couch on my stomach and reached my hand out for him. He folded his large body and sat in front of the couch with his back to me. I draped my arm across his chest.

"I'm a stay until you fall asleep. I'll lock up, although you can handle yourself, sharpshooter."

I smiled as I allowed the exhaustion to take hold before the sleeping pill could. "Thank you, Dizzy," I said, using the nickname that always brought a smile to his face.

WHEN I WOKE up the next morning, the sun blared through the half-closed blinds of my living room. I was covered with a duvet blanket. The pain in my head was as powerful as a hangover. I smiled because Walter had grabbed this blanket from Lance's and my bedroom. It must have been awkward for him to go in there. I kicked the cover off me because it reminded me of fucking Lance!

The moment I got my baby from my mother, I would get someone over to change the locks. That was it. I was done! Fuck him. I did everything in this house. He couldn't be bothered to make love to me, yet he could have a pseudo-sexual relationship with someone who referred to me as his ex-wife.

I'd show him an ex-wife all right. No more nice Brielle. I jumped up to do a two-step and laughed deviously. Pam, my hairstylist, would get an extra tip next week. I was pissed when she first suggested a postnuptial agreement. Besides, my marriage was blessed by God. Why would I need to plan for a breakup? Pam was the reason Lance wouldn't get a dime of my hard-earned money!

I picked up my phone to check on London. Whatever Chanté gave me knocked me out cold, because I didn't wake up until eleven a.m. I couldn't remember the last time I slept in since London had been born. I secretly envied other women whose husbands let them have days to sleep in. It was a luxury I wasn't afforded until I was away from London for work.

My chin trembled. Maybe people like me were destined for hard lives.

ME:

How is London?

WOMAN WHO GAVE ME LIFE:

It's about time. Call me NOW!

I wasn't a drinker, but I could use one, under the circumstances. I stood and stretched my body. My phone battery was almost dead. I had twenty missed calls from Lance. What could he possibly want to discuss? After I plugged my phone in, I found the app I used to hire contractors and quickly located the locksmith with the highest reviews. He said he could be at my house in less than an hour. *Perfect.*

CHANTÉ:

Don't text me if you're resting. Hopefully your phone is powered off. Let me know if you need help with my baby. *Kissing face emoji*

Before I could respond to her text, my phone rang loudly with an annoying fire siren noise. It was my mother's ringtone. I accepted the call only because my child was in her care.

"Where are you!" she yelled.

I pulled the phone back from my ear. I would have loved a supportive mother like the ones I saw on television, at this moment.

"I'm at home. I'm sorry I didn't call. I just woke up."

She was quiet for a moment. It was uncharacteristic for me to sleep until almost noon.

"Are you sick?"

I shook my head. I would be surprised if being under the weather would have changed her expectations for me. I was to perform, no matter what, because excuses were tools of incompetence.

"No, ma'am."

She said nothing.

"Lance and I... Lance and I had a fight, and I didn't want London around for it."

"All couples fight—"

"Not like this," I cut in. "This was not okay."

"Did he hit you?"

I sighed. Physical abuse was awful, but it wasn't the only reason for dissension.

"No, ma'am."

"Then come and get your child. You think you're the only one with problems, girl?"

"No. He just—"

"He just nothing. Get yourself up and dressed. I have things to do."

"I'll be there as soon as the locksmith leaves."

"The locksmith?"

"Yes. I'll see you no later than two."

I disconnected the call. For the umpteenth time, I silently thanked God for my chosen family. They had the capacity to hold space for me, while my blood relatives... they didn't.

Walt

HARD KNOCKS at my front door shook me from my restful state. I left Brielle's spot after one a.m. this morning, so there was no way I would make it to the office. Joi didn't mind. Her only inquiry was whether I'd made progress with the presentation for Zanaé's team. I assured her that Bree's pitch would knock her fancy socks off.

After our quick exchange, I went back to sleep. The knocks continued, and I prayed it wasn't who I thought it was. I stumbled out of bed, unable to check my phone. I'd forgotten to plug it in once I checked in with Joi. I opened my door bare chested and unbothered that my locs were in every direction. For several moments, the beautiful, insecure woman simply stared at me.

She let her light brown eyes skate over my form, and I wished her fierce attraction to me was enough to keep me interested. It wasn't. Melina was a stunning and talented social media manager for the local news station.

"I drove past and saw your car outside. Why aren't you at work?"

She peered past me to see if someone else was in my house. *I'm too damn old for this.* "Hello to you too, Melina."

"Don't try to play me. I called you when you stopped answering my texts. Did you block me?"

She rested her tiny wrist on her hip, and even though I couldn't stand a combative woman, I appreciated everything about her body. Because of her job, Melina was in good shape, and she always dressed nicely. She wore one of those skirts that started above her belly button and ended at her knee-high boots. Her chunky sweater was an inch too long and hung at the level of her knuckles.

It was a shame she was full of suspicion. We weren't exclusive. I was honest about my disinterest in monogamy from the beginning.

There was no need to sneak around just to spare her feelings. I didn't have the mental bandwidth for those games.

"My phone died."

She exhaled dramatically.

I rubbed a hand down my face. I didn't want to break up with her like this. I also didn't deserve to be spoken to and accused the way I was when I hadn't done anything.

"Melina, I was up late last night because Bree and Chanté needed—"

She clapped her hands. "Bree! I knew it. You swear she's your friend, but whenever you go silent, she's at the center of your universe."

"Calm down. I was at her place last night with Chanté. You got a problem with Chanté too? She's also one of my close friends."

"I trust her, and I trust that you don't want her."

"Look, I'm not about to stand here while you talk out of the side of your neck about my friends. Bree needed my help, and I didn't get enough sleep. Shit!"

"You don't help me, Walter. When do you ever help me?"

I laughed. I hadn't meant to laugh out loud, but I couldn't hide my shock. "You don't need my help, Melina. No shade, but you have a pampered princess lifestyle. There's nothing wrong with it, but you don't live like a single mother."

Melina's arms were folded across her chest. She wouldn't let this shit go. "Bree is married. How is she a single mother?"

My phone rang behind us.

"Don't answer that," she demanded.

I hesitated. Maybe I shouldn't get it, but if it was Brielle, I wanted to be available for her. I hung my head. "Do you want to come in?"

She scowled, then stormed off.

"Fuck!"

I closed the door and prayed that Melina and I could sit down and talk like two rational adults. There was no need for drama. All I wanted was to chill when we were together. Was that too much to ask?

Bree

THE SMIRK ON MY FACE WHEN LANCE TEXTED WAS PETTY, but I was at the point where I genuinely didn't care.

> LANCE:
>
> You changed the locks?!?

He hadn't cared about my feelings. For over a year, I prayed that my kindness would be enough. I made allowances and extended him grace he didn't deserve. During the brief moments when I doubted my decision to lock him out, I thought about what Lance did in our room. He'd done unspeakable acts in the bed we used to make love in. He betrayed me in the sacred space where I slept with our child or alone most nights.

Lance refused to touch me, but there was a familiarity in the way the online woman spoke. They weren't involved in a strictly sexual arrangement. If that was the case, why did she know about me? And the nerve of him to tell her I was his ex.

"Little girl." My mom snapped her fingers in front of my face.

"All the bills I pay around here," I muttered. The words just tumbled out of my mouth, and once they were released, I didn't want to take them back.

"Excuse me?" My mother wore that faux confused look on her face—the one that drove me nuts. She was much brighter than she pretended to be. This was the role placed on my shoulders when I was a child. I took whatever was served to me, and I did it with a cheerful disposition.

I gave my mom money out of guilt because she babysat for me. Between the three able bodied adults living there they had the means to cover the bills, but my mom had that secret shopping habit, and my brother never kept a job.

Lance's distance and indiscretion flipped a light switch for me. Why did I deserve bad treatment from the people who were supposed to love me the most?

"What did you just say to Mom?"

My oldest brother, Trevor, still lived at home. He was a forty-year-old man with two kids by two different mothers. I loved my brother, but it was a challenge to respect a grown man who still allowed people to call him TT. Trevor didn't work, and nobody questioned him about it.

Let me sleep in, and the world would topple upside down. There had always been a double standard at play when it came to me and my brothers, but the bullying would end today.

I grabbed London from his arms and smiled at my baby as I secured him in the booster chair I bought specifically for when he was here. I poured a handful of his favorite snack and passed him his spill proof cup. I stood and flung his diaper bag over my arm.

"I said, with all the bills I pay around here," I repeated slowly to Trevor. His eyes widened, but I refocused my attention on our mother. "I recognize your tone. When you call me a little girl, you make it seem like I'm irresponsible, even though I pay quite a few bills here. I love you, Mom, and I'm grateful for you watching London, but I'm sick of the way y'all treat me."

She gasped. Trevor went to speak, but I lifted my hand to stop him.

"When have I ever complained about giving any of y'all money?"

They looked at each other and then back at me.

"I'll wait." I was on a roll now.

I peeked over at London where he busied himself with the magnets on the tray attached to his seat. "Wait. Wait. Wait, Grammy," London chanted.

"I'm tired of everybody disrespecting me. First Lance, now this."

"What happened with Lance?" Trevor asked.

"TT, stay out of grown folks' business," our mother fussed.

I shook my head. He was five years older than me. Maybe if we could speak freely in this house, my brother would have warned me about my husband from the beginning. I chuckled to myself. My brother and Lance were the same, only Trevor hadn't married or moved in with either of his sponsors. The two mothers of his children paid for everything. They silently took his shit because at least he didn't hit them and at least he wasn't locked up.

Dustin was my other brother and the middle child. He was what some would call the forgotten child. Dustin left home the week he turned eighteen, and although he and I got along, I couldn't honestly say I didn't know him the way I knew Trevor. We didn't spend nearly enough time together.

"I need to go." I gathered my baby and his things. "Say bye, London."

He waved at his grandmother and uncle. "Bye, London."

It was hard to stay mad with that angel by my side.

I GOT London down for a nap just as an email alerted me that The Lone Wolf posted another article. It was entitled, *"Are Black men the new wife? Why black women struggle to couple."*

I gasped and read the article as I held my breath.

There's a new generation of Black men—who for many reasons aren't providing for themselves nor their families. Our women suffer when they are forced to step out of their femininity and shoulder responsibilities they weren't designed for. This has nothing to do with whether a woman works outside the home. It has everything to do with expecting them to have several full-time jobs.

Cleaning, cooking, and homemaking are several jobs. Raising children is a full-time job. As men, we've missed the mark. Just because some of our mothers had no other choice but to hustle doesn't mean she should have. It's unsustainable. Somewhere along the line, roles have been reversed.

Boatloads of Black men currently stay home while their wives and girlfriends are the breadwinners of the household. Again, there are many families where the man is temporarily unemployed. Until he's back on his feet, he holds the house down. This article isn't about them. It's about families where the gifted Black woman is exploited because of her seemingly effortless ability to earn. A good deal of these women are miserable and exhausted.

Meanwhile, their male partners are kept. Black women need real help, not wives. My advice to women is to find a man who will grind for you and treat you with the care you deserve. This advice is not for the Primadona women who claim to be above eating at chain restaurants. Bless their hearts. They can have a dedicated article later.

To the burned-out Black women, you have all the power in the world and in your relationship. You get to change your mind. You decide who is worthy to be in your space and who you financially support. You deserve better. I personally don't believe in marriage, but I believe you deserve a husband, not a wife.

I'd subscribed to Walter's blog many moons ago. This was the first time I was called out by it. Under his pseudonym, he wrote about his experience which regularly included the people around him. I read his last article about black children in school. It was undoubtedly inspired by the conversation Chanté had with us about Hakeem.

Was Lance my wife?

LANCE:

We have to talk eventually

Argh! After reading Walt's words, the mere sight of Lance's name on my caller ID made my lip snarl. I wasn't ready to officially leave him, but I was open to the idea of returning the energy he'd given me. Maybe a hall pass wasn't a bad idea after all. I grabbed my phone just as I saw London waking from his nap on the monitor.

WALT AND CHANTÉ BESTIE GROUP CHAT:

I'll do it

CHANTÉ:

the freaky sneaky weekend?!?

I chuckled at her response and how quickly she hit me back.

WALT:

you got two weeks before Florida. Hope
you ready, Bree Bree

CHANTÉ:

oh she'll be ready. My best friend is gonna
be fine as fuck when I get done with her.

Flutters rumbled deep in my belly. I smirked as I made my way to my baby. *What did I sign up for?* I got London's diaper changed, just as the doorbell rang.

"Dada," London said.

If I wasn't completely obsessed with my baby, I'd be creeped out by his Spidey senses. He had this innate ability to know who was at the door or who was on the phone before I did, and he always guessed right.

"You wanna get it?" I asked.

He nodded and toddled toward the door. By the time I caught up with him, his little hand twisted the knob back and forth unsuccessfully. I peered through the peephole, and sure enough, it was London's father. I picked him up and cracked the door wide enough for Lance to see us but said nothing.

London leaned forward, and I allowed him to go into his father's arms.

"Hey, man! Daddy misses you," Lance sang.

London laughed, but I was on the verge of tears. Why did Lance do this to us? I couldn't bear to have him anywhere near me, yet we were bonded together for a lifetime. We shared an amazing son who needed both of us. Once London got his fill, he wiggled out of Lance's grip and focused his attention on a new pile of leaves in our spacious front yard. I grabbed a coat for both of us and moved beyond the door.

"I'm sorry."

I blinked back tears. What the hell did he expect me to say? I accept? *I* wanted out, but I wasn't sure that was what God wanted. He'd cheated as far as I was concerned.

Was our relationship even salvageable? What would happen if I went through with the hall pass? There would certainly be no coming back from that.

"Did you sleep with her?"

Lance's shoulders sagged. His eyes were everywhere except on me. An innocent man would have denied it right away. *I should have shot him when I had the chance.* These days, I didn't recognize my own savage thoughts. Lance's behavior triggered the kill switch.

I didn't know what came over me, but I reared back and slapped him. London was preoccupied, thank God. He hadn't seen me pimp slap his daddy. It wasn't just online. He cheated on me for real.

My pulse quickened, and the world spun a bit faster. He didn't even have the balls to come clean. Like always, I had to pry it out of him. What exactly was he sorry for?

"Did you bring that woman to my house?"

"No."

I wasn't relieved by his response at all.

"I'll stay outside with London if you want to grab some clothes. We can't stay together in the house. I don't trust myself." Once again, I was startled by my own voice. Good girl Brielle had left the chat.

"Do whatever you want, babe. Hit me, curse me out, just don't leave me," he pleaded.

Lance usually took my breath away. Each time I saw him, I was physically drawn to him—even when he no longer wanted to make love. He had a captivating face that was a carbon copy of our son's, but I couldn't appreciate it today. He was pathetic.

I stared at him as ice coursed through my veins. "I'm not leaving. You are." I maintained eye contact with my soon-to-be ex-husband as I stepped away from the door and into the grass with my baby love. I sat cross-legged with him as he stomped on the colorful, crunchy leaves that had fallen due to the change of season.

Lance heaved a breath. He went into the house and gathered his belongings. After fifteen minutes or so, he emerged with an oversized suitcase.

"Can I see y'all over the weekend?" he asked once he'd loaded his car—a car that was in my name.

"Feel free to come back and take London with you."

Disappointment crowded his watchful eyes. He lifted our son and pressed a kiss to his pudgy cheek.

"Dada. Bye bye." He pointed at Lance's car and leaned toward the grass where he once again wanted to play.

I stood and crossed my arms. "I'm going to Florida for a week. Can you keep London, or should I leave him with my mom?"

"I can check with my mom. That's where I'm staying, B." He waited for me to respond, but I couldn't care less if he stayed under the 405 Freeway with the other bums. My teeth were gritted so tight that my jaw ached.

"I'm sure she won't have a problem with it," he amended.

I wasn't ready for my baby to have extended visits at my mother-in-law's home without me. There was no telling what she'd say around him. This was the part of breaking up I wasn't prepared for. My nostrils flared because I hadn't done this to us. He did.

I pulled London close the moment Lance headed for the driveway. He stiffened and wailed in protest.

Lance turned back toward us, lowering himself to London's height and pinching his cheeks. "Come to daddy." London relaxed and did as his father asked. "Be nice to mommy, okay?" he whispered.

London nodded as tears wet his cheeks. "Dada phone."

Just as my wall started to dissolve at the fatherly moment I'd just witnessed, I saw a picture of the woman from the live stream on Lance's phone. I snatched it from him. Panic washed over my soon-to-be ex-husband's face.

"Hello?"

"Who is this?" Emma asked in a thick Italian accent. The name Emma was programmed into his phone with a peach emoji, an Italian flag, and a South African flag. She was mixed.

"This is Lance's wife. Who is this?" I had no intention of taking

Lance's ass back. It would take a divine intervention and a complete 180 on his part for me to even consider it, but she didn't need to know that. My insecurities about Lance's attraction to me were at an all-time high. The woman was so fair-skinned I originally thought she was white.

"Lance is single. You must be Brielle, Lance's ex-wife." She stressed every syllable of the words she spoke. If I wasn't on the verge of homicide, I would have found her voice soothing.

"Baby," Lance tried.

My eyes flew to him.

"You, B. I'm calling you baby. I haven't answered any of her calls. I told her I want my family back."

"Does she know that?" I asked through gritted teeth. I feared I would break a tooth if I didn't relax.

"Do I know what? What your bedroom looks like? What Lance's penis smells like?"

She'd gotten what he deprived me of. My body shook when the phone slipped from my hands. *I have to keep it together for London.* I turned to grab my son and held him tightly while he kicked to be returned to the grass. I couldn't bring myself to face Lance again.

I meant it when I said I didn't trust myself around him. Had the two of them been together in my house physically, I would have shot them both. I entered the house and slammed the door behind me.

Walt

I'M MEETING Zanaé this weekend. It was the Monday before our work trip, and I had no idea how I would concentrate on anything with the way my mind was preoccupied. It had been two weeks since I'd last spoken to Melina after she left my house in the middle of our conversation. She convinced herself that if I answered my phone, I was somehow choosing my best friend over her.

I'd forgotten I had Bree and Chanté's text message alerts set to ring so I wouldn't miss them. Melina had stormed off because of a text. Bree announced in the group chat that she was onboard with the hall pass after all. In hindsight, it was a message that could have waited. Melina and I needed to find common ground, and we needed to do that shit soon if we stood a chance. I opened my phone and called her.

"Hello?" she answered in an annoyed tone.

"Is that how you greet your ex?" I teased.

"What?"

"You don't tend to me, and after this weekend when I meet Zanaé, I might let her lock me down."

Melina's light giggles drifted through my phone. "You wish."

"I'm serious. I'm pitching to Zanaé in Florida this weekend, and you better not post about it."

"Not even anonymously?"

"I'm telling you I'm going to be face-to-face with Zanaé—the international pop star icon with a voice like a mermaid and a body like a goddess—and you want to post about it?"

"I thought your crush on her was innocent. Now..." she started.

"Now what?"

"Now that she's going to see you in person, I'm a little worried."

"As you should be," I teased.

"I'm serious. You look like every male model she uses in her videos. You're huge, and you have those hooded eyes that make women crazy."

"Speaking of crazy—"

"I know you didn't just call me crazy."

"I'm only half joking. I'm serious about us figuring this out though. You showed up to my mom's house unannounced and questioned her about something we already discussed."

"Every time I turn around, you're blowing me off for Brielle, and I saw your blog about black men being the new wife. That shit was about her and me," she responded, ignoring my statement about her popping up at my mom's spot.

"Not everything is about you, Melina."

"So, it was for her?"

I rubbed my head. This woman had a body like I'd never seen, and when she wasn't acting like a psycho, she was fun to be with. Why the hell was she so damn crazy?

"It wasn't for her, but it was about women like her."

"Walt Dizzy," Brielle sang as she stormed into my office. "Hang it up. Whoever it is can wait. I have our resort information for Florida."

"What did she say?"

My face twitched, and Bree slapped her hand over her mouth. "Is that Melina?" I loved Bree, but she couldn't whisper for shit.

"It is Melina!" She yelled into my ear like Bree could hear her. "You're staying with her for a week?"

"We work together, Melina. Of course we'll both be there."

"You know what, Walt? I'm done."

"You're done?" My voice had risen three octaves. She waited two weeks to do this shit over the phone.

"I'm not going to sit around and compete with your best friend. It's obvious to everybody, except you and her, that there's sexual tension between you. Urgh!"

"She hung up." I peered at my phone to ensure the call was disconnected. It was.

"She didn't know I would be in Florida?" Bree's eyes were wide.

I hated endings to relationships like the one I just had with Melina. I preferred a clean break where each person's thoughts were clearly communicated. She said she was done, so that was that. It irritated the shit out of me that Melina gave me no time to speak my piece, but it was hard to stay in a bad mood with Brielle's cheerful one. Sad Bree weighed heavy on my heart. I was helpless to change her situation other than lending her a listening ear.

"She does now." I smirked at her, and her shoulders relaxed.

"Barging in has never been an issue for us. I'm sorry, Walter."

"She broke up with me."

Bree's hand flew to her chest as she plopped down in a chair. "I feel awful. Call her back."

"You crazy as hell. And say what?"

"You really need to stop calling women crazy." Bree rolled her eyes and opened the laptop balanced on her knees.

"You sound like Melina."

She glared at me then returned to her computer. She propped it up on my desk and spun it in my direction.

"This is where Joi set us up!" Bree squealed. The dimple in her chin showed itself and made me laugh.

I almost choked when I saw the *Carnelian Resort and Spa*. The luxury getaway was known as a retreat for the rich and famous. It was low key, with very few pictures of the comings and goings of its guests on social media. Aside from its reputation as a covert escape for the elite, its modern and sexy aesthetic was hashtag goals for anyone seeking a true baecation.

I jumped up to get a closer look. "Say you lyin'."

Bree giggled. "I swear. Joi saw me walk past her office and said to dress accordingly." Brielle's smile faded.

"What?" I swiped her laptop. The more I considered the magnitude of our assignment, the more it made sense for us to be at the *Carnelian*. We were going to meet Zanaé who was used to five-star treatment.

"I don't have anything to wear. I'm in need of a vacation, but I don't have an article of clothing in my closet that says I'm ready to mingle."

My head snapped in her direction.

"What?" Her brows were knitted together as she searched my face for answers.

"You texted us that you wanted to do it, but I'm surprised to hear good girl Bree Bree say she's ready to mingle."

"He didn't just cheat online. He slept with her."

I set her laptop down and rounded my desk to close the door to my office.

"How you know?" Bree deserved better than Lance, but he was her husband. She wanted it to work, so when she explained what happened the night she caught him with the webcam chick, I admitted that most men didn't consider what Lance did cheating. I hesitated to share the notion with her because whether he cheated or not, she was still better than him.

"He came to the house last week." She shook her head and collected her laptop. "He agreed to keep London while we're gone."

My eyes were wide. Bree was sensitive about her marriage. As one of her best friends, I was tasked with toeing the line between having her back and supporting her choices, even though I didn't support who she'd chosen.

She had her hand on the doorknob when I added, "Don't worry about clothes. Chanté can't wait to get her hands on you." I winked at her when she turned to face me.

"Thanks, Dizzy."

After Bree left, I was uneasy. It was my idea for her to take the hall pass, but when she said she was ready to mingle, it didn't sit right with me. I stood and peered out of my tenth-floor office window.

I'd already watched Lance drag Brielle down; how the hell was I going to stomach some new clown in her space? Not to be deterred, I called Chanté.

"What's wrong with Bree?" Chanté asked flustered.

"Nothing bad."

"Oh, you scared me. I almost knocked my boss over," Chanté added, winded like she'd run to accept my call. I generally didn't call her directly. I respected her man and didn't make reaching out a habit unless it was about Bree.

"Brielle said, and I quote, she's ready to mingle. She showed me the resort and got bent out of shape because she doesn't have anything to wear."

"I got her covered."

"I know you do. Are you and Chase coming?"

"Yes! And I can't wait."

"Me either. Me and Chase can keep an eye on her."

"Walter Disney Simmons, are you worried?" Her voice had the same sing-song tone Bree used when she made fun of me.

I did a lap around my office because I couldn't sit still.

"A little. She's a good girl. Y'all both are, but at least you got Chase."

"Mm hmm. Well, Bree will have all three of us watching her back. I need to call my bestie now so we can get this makeover poppin'. Get off my phone, Simmons."

Before I could respond, she hung up.

———

I LEFT the office because my head was a jumbled mess. Between irrational fantasies about Zanaé and worry about Brielle's safety, I couldn't focus on shit. Just as I propped my phone into the car dock, my father's number appeared on the screen. My nostrils flared as I gripped the steering wheel until my normally brown knuckles were white. Unless there was something wrong with my mama, there was no need for us to speak.

I ignored his call and peeled out of the parking garage. As I turned corners in pursuit of my house, my mind searched for explanations. How could incredible women like my mother and Brielle waste time with men like my father and Lance? It had been almost a year since I spoke to him last. My father and I couldn't make it through a conversation without it leading to a blow up.

My head throbbed by the time I made it home. The property was in a rapidly growing subdivision that I'd been lucky to get in on before the prices skyrocketed to where they were now. Although I was never fully invested in any house that wasn't my mother's, it was the home I built and had come to provide the respite I needed after days like today.

I tossed my belongings on a small table in the foyer and stepped out of my shoes. Melina hated when I undressed at the door, but she wasn't here now. Clothes were restricting, and my bedroom was too far to wait.

My water bill was sky high because of the ridiculously long showers I took. It was my meditative time. Melina was on my mind because what my mom said was true. Everyone wasn't raised like me.

The two of us had a different set of values, but I didn't want to hurt her because of how I chose to live my life. Melina would make someone a happy man. I just wasn't that guy. She demanded to be treated like a princess, and I couldn't breathe without respect. Her accusations of me putting Bree ahead of her weren't completely inaccurate though.

There was never anything sexual between me and Bree, but she was my best friend. If Melina forced me to choose, that was a battle she'd lose every time. What was insane was how she was more preoccupied with Brielle than Zanaé. I would risk it all for Zanaé's fine ass, and Aiden was right to hate. All I needed was five minutes with her, and I could seal the deal.

Before I left the office, I pulled up her social media and liked a gang of her pictures. It was some high school level stalking that I wasn't ashamed of.

I stepped out of my shower, finally calm. I dressed in sweats and a T-shirt and grabbed a beer from the fridge. Since Melina wouldn't take my calls and I was alone for the night, I parked myself in front of my dining room table and worked on the unfinished one-thousand-piece puzzle of a beautiful landscape.

Bree

THE *BROWN BADDIES BOOK CLUB* MET ONCE A MONTH AT AN eatery a few miles from my neighborhood. Last year, I was in the bookstore with a disengaged Lance when I saw several women seated in a cozy corner with the same book. I made my way over and told them how much I enjoyed it. They invited me to stay, and since Lance was thrilled for an excuse to leave, I joined on the spot.

This month, we were to read *A Naughty Rendezvous*. It was an annoyingly relatable book. The main female character, Jada, wanted to spruce up her sex life, but her husband wasn't interested. While my morals wouldn't support cheating of any kind, I found myself on fire as I read the details of her one o'clock appointments with Odell. The worst part was that Jada's husband started to come around, but she continued to meet with her sneaky link.

I flopped down in a chair with a huff.

"Everything OK, Bree?" Eve asked.

She was one of the founders of the Brown Baddies. Even though

I only had two best friends, she and I spoke freely about our families and work. We'd gotten close through sharing our perspectives on literature.

"I didn't finish this book."

Eve's eyes were wide. "Why not?"

"I couldn't get with the whole affair trope. Javon wasn't emotionally available, but he was trying, and Jada kept sneaking around with Odell. Some of us wish we had a man like Javon. He's the financial breadwinner, he cares about their children, and he notices when she changes her hair."

Eve wore a smirk when she said, "There's a plot twist, sis. Denise Essex did her thing with this one. You know I support anybody's decision not to finish a book, but it isn't what you think."

Lauren and Kori joined our table.

"I can't wait to talk about Odell." Lauren gushed.

Eve held up her hand. "We can't."

"Why not?" Kori asked with her hand propped on her hip.

"Little Miss Church Girl marked it DNF because she doesn't believe in cheating on a good man," Eve teased.

The three of them eyed each other, then fell into boisterous laughter.

"What did I miss?" If they thought adultery was funny, I needed to rethink who I spent my time with. London was with Chanté whenever I did my monthly book club outings, but if this was how we'd spend our time, I preferred to be with him.

"Girl, you need to finish this book and you'll understand. Don't you have a trip coming up this weekend? Read it on the flight," Lauren insisted.

"I do. I have a question for y'all," I mumbled.

Kori scooted her chair closer. "Why do I get the impression this is about to be better than the book?" she probed with interested eyes.

She and Lauren high-fived. These women were professionals like me. They had families and a million responsibilities. This book club was our refuge. It was where we could fully be ourselves. When we met up, we were vulnerable, free, and most of all, messy.

"I have a friend," I started.

"Of course you do," Eve countered. "I wish they had wine here." She gazed down at her coffee, disappointed.

Lauren elbowed her and gave me her full attention.

"Her treacherous friends know she doesn't have a good man like Javon, so they want her to take a hall pass."

Kori choked on her water.

"Are you OK?" I pressed.

She raised her hands and swatted Lauren's pats away. "Bitch, this is way better than the book. A hall pass, like sleep with somebody other than your husband, then go back like nothing ever happened?" Kori was happily married, as far as I could tell, but like Jada from *A Naughty Rendezvous*, she and her man had been together for almost twenty years. Part of the reason she read romance was to escape into taboo situations she would never act out in her real life.

I nodded. "If she has an experience that's strictly about getting her sexual needs met, maybe she could face the work needed to put her marriage back together."

"Wait, she's having problems in her marriage?" Eve's tone lost its playfulness.

I nodded again.

"Let's vote," Lauren said. "I'll go first." She raised her hand high. "She should have the filthiest hall pass of her wildest dreams."

Kori raised her hand in agreement. "Yup. What she said."

A weak smile covered my lips. We all stared at Eve who was silent.

"What?" I asked her.

"This changes everything. Problems in a marriage don't justify a hall pass. If things were good and they both decided they were OK with it, that would be different. I'm still not sure it's a great idea for real life, although it would make for a juicy book." Eve directed her gaze toward me as she continued. "You said your friend is having problems in her marriage. She's out of her mind if she thinks sex with a stranger is going to motivate her to return home and repair an already failing situation. If anything, she's going to further complicate things."

"Seems like it worked for Jada," I muttered.

"Finish the book," Kori and Lauren sang.

"Look, sis, I don't know how close you are with this friend, but if she's going to go through with it, she needs to be ten toes down. It's her life. If she wants to explore, she should, but she may not want her husband after a new man puts it on her," Lauren emphasized.

I stood. "I'm gonna go." This was a conversation I should have with Chanté. Why had I even brought it up? If I were insane enough to go back and salvage what I had with Lance, the last thing I would need is questions from the Brown Baddies.

"Aww, man," Kori said to my back. Before anyone could ask anything else, I was outside the door to the bookstore.

The cool January air hit my face and sent a chill through my opened coat. This was my life, and I made the decisions from here on out. I couldn't be sure if it was Lance's cheating or all my unacknowledged years of playing it safe that gave me this new courage. I did what I was supposed to do. I was a good wife, and I still hadn't hit Lance with the divorce papers he deserved.

As I shuffled to my car, my mind drifted to my best friend. Chanté offered to help me with clothes the moment Walter told her about the Florida trip. I'd been so adamant that a hall pass was cheating that I hadn't taken her up on it. Things were different now. Wasn't I justified?

I navigated to the screen with the contacts highlighted as favorites on my phone. Why wasn't Lance's name first? Why weren't either of my parents' names there? My stomach lurched. Had Trevor told my dad how I spoke to him and my mother? My father, Deacon Timothy Barnes, was a respected member of the church I attended as a child. He didn't tolerate disrespect.

Despite his futile attempts at spiritual bypassing, our relationship was as strained as my marriage. I longed for the type of relationship Walt had with his mother and Chanté had with her parents. Some of my favorite people belonged in leadership positions in the church, but my parents were two-faced. They loved my brothers and me in public but belittled us in private. That was why the only two contacts in the favorite list on my phone were Chanté and Walt.

I commanded my digital assistant to dial Walt Dizzy.

"Bree Bree! What up?" Walt bellowed into the phone.

"You sound funny. What's wrong with you?" I pressed.

I was enroute to pick up London. Chanté would probably curse me out for waiting days before the trip to get my life together, but my conversation with the Brown Baddies struck a chord deep within me. I would not be made to feel bad for thinking of myself for once. Lance hadn't prioritized our marriage. He ought to be thankful I hadn't shot him.

"You do too."

"You go first," we said simultaneously.

"*Ladies* first," he added.

"Argh! I was at the bookstore—"

"With Lauren's fine ass?"

I could hear his smirk through the phone.

"Yes. She said I needed to be ten toes down if I did the hall pass, but Eve disagreed."

"What do you want, Brielle?"

I sat silent as I considered Walter's question. What *did* I want? I asked myself what Lance would want? I'd contemplated what was best for my marriage? I'd even considered how a separation would affect London. Not once had I asked myself what I wanted.

A horn blared behind me. I was at a light that turned green during my deep contemplation.

"Oh, sheesh. Sorry!" I said with a wave in my rearview mirror like the person behind me could hear.

"I don't know, Dizzy."

"I bet you do. You're just afraid of being judged. Fuck what anyone else thinks, Bree. You deserve to let your hair down in Florida. Don't be a camel for one weekend," he teased.

"Whatever. Your turn."

"Mason Frazier called my phone today." Walter's voice was barely above a whisper.

Dizzy's father, Mason Frazier, was abusive to his mother. He'd opened up to me about it when we were in college. We were walking on campus and witnessed a guy grab his girlfriend's arm. When Walt saw the display of aggression, he flipped out. I had to drag him off the guy because I was afraid he'd get arrested. He never told anyone about the abuse he witnessed, including his father who had only hit Grace when Walter was supposed to be asleep.

"Did you answer?"

"Hell no."

"Do you think maybe it's time?"

He released a ragged breath. "Enough heavy shit. Where you at? I don't hear London Bridges wreaking havoc."

"I like how you made me spill then swerved when it was on you. I'm on the way to Chanté's so she can beautify me."

"Is that right? Is Chase really coming?"

"Yes, why?"

"Because the two of us are gonna have to vet whoever is on the receiving end of this hall pass of yours."

"What? I don't need a babysitter," I said, mortified.

"Yeah, you do."

I huffed into the phone. "I'm here." I rolled my eyes because I didn't need Walter, Chanté, and Chase to see me crash and burn. I hadn't had sex with anyone other than Lance in years. I didn't have a clue about how to pick up a man. I still got hit on regularly, but I wasn't interested in letting any of those men take me home.

"Get cute, and I'll see you in Florida."

"Bye, Dizzy."

I hustled to the front door with my hands cupped in front of my face. *Where did I leave my gloves?* The door swung open, and Hakeem, who was a beautiful mashup of his mother and father, answered the door.

"Hi, Auntie. Are you taking London already?"

I pulled him in for a hug. "Hey, nephew. I'm going to chat with your mom for a second, and then we'll have to leave, unfortunately."

Chase appeared at Hakeem's side with London in his arms. My heart leaped. Chase was a phenomenal husband *and* father. It was impossible for my broken heart not to compare my marriage to theirs. Chase worshiped the ground Chanté walked on. He executed both roles imperfectly, just as my friend deserved.

"Mama," London sang. He leaned his heavy body in my direction, and luckily, I braced myself to catch him.

"Hi, boo boo," I cooed. "Did he give you any trouble?" I asked Chase as I kissed London's cheek.

"He had a good time trying to keep up with Hakeem. You coming in?"

"Yeah, I need to speak to Chanté."

London wiggled out of my arms and did his best to keep up with Hakeem. "I'm going to the playroom until you're done talking to Mom," he shrieked. He grabbed a remote for a car that London trailed down the hall.

I stepped inside and allowed Chase to take my coat. "How are you holding up?" he asked.

I fought back tears. Chase's and Walter's questions were basic, but I was much more comfortable being the one asking than answering.

"Hey, girl. You're early. What happened?" Chanté cut in.

"I'll leave y'all to it," Chase said. He leaned down and kissed his wife, then whispered into her ear. She blushed, and I looked away. They'd been married for ten years, but they carried on like newlyweds.

Chase threw a nod in my direction and headed toward the playroom.

"What was that about?" I asked Chanté as I sat in her front room. The black accent wall pulled the entire space together. Despite my major hesitations of having nice decor with small children, Chanté's light gray sectional and mixed colored pillows was where we parked to catch up. It was the soft lighting on the end tables and the faux tea lights that added to the intimacy of her home.

"He's just being nasty about this weekend. He snooped and ran across my bathing suit." She fanned herself and winked at me.

"About that. Joi has Dizzy and I staying at the *Carnelian*. I don't have anything to wear."

Chanté's eyes bulged, and she swallowed dramatically. "OK.

There's no need to panic. I can handle this. We're fine," she said more to herself than to me.

In school, we called Chanté the hostess with the mostest. She had an undeniable gift of planning events and decorating homes. I'd attended Chanté's holiday parties more than I returned home to my parents' that time of year. She was skilled at making everyone feel included without doing too much. She wasn't performative, and she didn't expect anyone else to be a curated version of themselves in her presence.

Chanté's sense of style was unmatched. I spent most of my time in college wearing sweatpants. Chanté was like a character from the teen movie *Clueless*. She helped me plan my wedding and decorate several rooms in my house. I was confident she could make me hall pass ready.

She scrolled her phone and squealed when an alert came through.

"I told Janessa this was urgent. She can squeeze you in tomorrow, but you must be there first thing in the morning."

Before I could agree, Chanté continued.

"As soon as you can get away from work, meet me downtown by the McHaven Boutiques. We may have to devote a few hours, but we'll cover all your bases." She had barely taken a breath.

"Do I want to know what that means?"

I stood and grabbed my coat. I would get a good night's sleep since I needed to get up early for my hair appointment. She shook her head. "You always help Walt and I when we need it. You're kind and thoughtful, and you're an amazing mother. It's time… for you… to get *laid*, bitch!"

Chanté was a nut. She'd clapped while she spoke, to emphasize her words.

"What does get laid mean?" Hakeem stood at the entryway to

the front room as he asked the question with an introspective look on his youthful face.

My eyes bulged, and her head flew in his direction. "I didn't hear you come in, Keem."

"Is this a grown folks' conversation?" he asked.

I slapped my hand over my mouth to conceal my laughter.

"Yes, it is, but I love that you ask such good questions. That's why you're so smart."

Hakeem ran over and gave me a hug. "Bye, Auntie."

"Bye, handsome."

London toddled in and clapped his hands. "Keem."

My smile widened. I leaned down to pick up my baby. "Time to say bye."

"Outside." London pointed at the door.

As I bundled London up and gathered his things, Chanté hugged us both. "I'm going to text you her address and your appointment time. Don't be late, and please let her do what she does best."

"Fine." I breathed deeply. This was what I signed up for. It was time for me to loosen my grip and relax my standards. If all else failed and I got cold feet, at least I'd have a banging hair style.

* * *

Walt

I WAS IN A MOOD. Aiden was in my office like he was Joi's Pitbull. He went on and on about the itinerary for the coming weekend and next week.

"You and Brielle are on the same flight, of course. While the two of you are living it up at the *Carnelian*, the rest of us will be clear across town."

"Brielle?" My mouth dropped open.

"Yes, Walter. You and Brielle are the chosen ones this time. Your secret pitch for Zanaé had better be good."

Bree had always been attractive. I told her that on more than one occasion, but since she met Lance and had her baby, her appearance hadn't been her top priority. None of that took away from her natural beauty, because Brielle Kari Barnes had a spirit that drew people in. There was nothing more appealing than a good woman.

Today, she stole the breath from my lungs. She changed her hair, and I had to admit she was as fine as the day I met her back in college.

"I'm Walt," I said as I held the door open for a thick brown-skinned, bright-eyed freshman. She couldn't have been more than eighteen. She was the finest girl I'd seen since I'd stepped foot on campus. If I had to guess, based solely on the way she carried herself, I'd say she was a preacher's kid saving her virginity for Jesus. She had no idea how bad she really was.

"Hey." She peered up at me and scrunched her nose up.

"What's that look for?" I took the gigantic moving box from her hand and held the door for another lost freshman.

"Are you a senior?"

"Damn. Why? Do I look old or something? What's your name, girl?"

"Brielle. How old are you, Walter?"

"I said my name was Walt, and I'm twenty-two." I waited for her to tell me to step off like all the other girls her age. Just because I started college older than the traditional student didn't mean I was a creep.

"So, you're a super senior?" she teased.

"I'm a non-traditional freshman."

She exhaled and her shoulders relaxed. "Finally, somebody interested in a conversation that doesn't involve my favorite sexual position."

My mouth dropped open, but I bounced back quickly. "How you know that's not what time I'm on?"

She shifted her weight into her popped hip and regarded me. Brielle was a beautiful breath of fresh air. There was chemistry between us, but I didn't reduce her to her appearance like I did with the other women I'd met. She was the type of girl I would marry if I believed in that.

"Because your mama raised you right. Carry this to my room."

I nodded and followed. If any other woman spoke to me the way she did, I would have been pissed. I didn't mind with her. Brielle was fine, but she hit the nail on the head as far as my intentions. Her aura was unlike anything I'd ever experienced. I wanted to be around her in whatever capacity she would have me.

HER NATURAL HAIR was out in a full curly 'fro that touched her shoulders. It was dyed from her normal jet-black color to a sandy brown. The new color made her lightly toasted skin pop. Bree had new bangs that highlighted her pouty lips and slightly upturned nose.

"Drool much?" Aiden muttered, interrupting the trance Brielle's new look put me in. He followed my eyeline where Bree stood with her face buried in her computer.

"This itinerary is ridiculous." She huffed. "Have you seen it?" Her gaze collided with mine, and I was physically unable to tear my eyes from her face.

The sides of her lips lifted. She fluffed her hair and swayed. "Is it too much?"

"Hell nah," I shrieked.

"Brielle! Look at you trying to steal Zanaé's shine. Everything about this new vibe is winning." Aiden gave Bree a once over, then whispered, "Your *friend* is over there drooling," he muttered as he left my office.

I cleared my throat. "He's right. You're fine as hell, Bree Bree."

A blush covered her round cheeks. "Thank you, Walter. Chanté had her hairdresser hook me up. She said I was hall pass ready."

My jaw tightened. I was the one who insisted she put herself out there and get her needs taken care of. Now I wasn't convinced it was such a good idea. I couldn't find the words to say, and that never happened when I was with Brielle. It was one of my favorite things about having two female best friends. I could be vulnerable without fear that it would somehow make me less of a man.

I'd already admitted she was fine, but I found myself wanting to say it again.

"You're doing that thing," she said when she sashayed in my direction. Her heels were new. They were sexier than what she normally wore.

"What thing?" I pulled one of her curls and watched it bounce back like a spring.

"The lip to nose thing where you rub your lip against your nose like you're in deep thought. What's got you in your head?"

You!

I stepped back and rounded my desk to create distance between us but also to get an unobstructed view of her. *What the hell is wrong with me?*

"Nothing. Just thinking about what I'm going to do when I get a hold of Zanaé," I lied.

She rolled her eyes. "Ugh! You're disgusting." She turned around, and I found myself admiring her ass. *The hell?*

"You got new clothes?" Sweat beaded on my brow at the marvelous sight.

"Yeah. You like?" She put her hands on her knees and twerked. It was as though I'd forgotten how attractive Bree really was. Her skirt was form-fitting but was stretchy enough for her cheeks to shake. I needed to get some ass if I was checking out my best friend.

"I do."

"Chanté made sure I had something for every occasion, including business casual for our meetings."

"Why are you wearing it here?" I willed myself not to do the lip to nose thing she so eloquently called me out for.

"Because these are for McHaven. The ones for Florida are sheer. Weather appropriate," she said with a wink.

Shit!

six

Bree

MY STOMACH WAS IN KNOTS. OUR FLIGHT WAS SET TO LEAVE this afternoon, and I needed to head to the airport if I didn't want to be late. London was asleep in the back seat next to his diaper bag and Monster Truck suitcase. This wasn't right. Why did I have to travel for work while Lance could see London anytime he wanted?

Maybe Lance is my wife. I pouted in the car then spoke to my baby as though he could hear me.

"Mama has to leave you with daddy and your grandmother. I pray you'll be safe physically, emotionally, and that you have a good time. You need your daddy, even if I don't."

I fought back tears because I wouldn't show fear in his father's presence. The last thing I needed was for Lance to watch me fall apart without him. I unbuckled myself, and just as I'd freed London from his seat, Lance appeared beside the car.

"I got it," he said as he retrieved London and his bags.

Damn! Lance being helpful? I must be seeing things.

"I'll have my cell with me most of the time. If it's an emergency, you have the number to the resort."

"You're really going to meet Zanaé?"

I nodded. I was geeked about the opportunity but loathed the need to converse with Lance.

"I like what you did with your hair," he said. He hesitated because I'd become unpredictable. The last time we saw each other, I'd slapped him.

"I can't believe you noticed," slipped out before I could stop it.

"Look—"

"Don't. Thank you, but don't. I just want a cordial handoff."

Lance shifted and steadied his breath before he spoke. "You can come in and see where he's sleeping," he offered.

"I appreciate that more than you know, but I'm afraid if I do, I won't make it on this trip." Water crowded my eyes.

Lance set London's things down and handed him back to me. "You know you want to," he teased.

I squeezed London to the point that he woke up. "I love you, London."

"Mama, byyyyyye," he said in a sleepy voice. It was his way of saying I was about to leave. I kissed his full cheeks and handed him back to Lance. I turned to leave before I fell apart.

"I'll send you pics, B."

"Thank you, Lance."

I got in my car and blasted my praise and worship music on the drive to the airport, although I planned to sleep with someone other than my husband. I didn't care what my mom and dad thought when it came to their interpretation of a good Christian. My God wanted me to be free. I should probably wait until I was no longer tethered to Lance, but I wasn't perfect. As my favorite church mom used to say, 'I didn't crawl up on a cross and die.'

The music soothed my nerves. I surrendered my fears about

London's safety. Whether I did or didn't do the hall pass, I turned over the need to know exactly what would happen. Instead, I would allow myself to rest from incessant worrying and stressing. This was a trip for me to impress our mega famous client and to enjoy my time to get my needs met for once—even if that meant a week of good, uninterrupted sleep.

The airport was crowded, and the jovial mood I was in when I arrived evaporated. Everyone was in a hurry, and manners took a back seat. News stations blared in the background, pushing fear as their drug of choice. As an emphatic soul, I absorbed all the energy around me.

I made it through the security check and wished Chanté could have flown with me. She and Chase wouldn't arrive until later this evening. I hadn't spoken to Walter but remembered he and I were supposed to be on the same flight. I sat at a bar to grab a drink and fished for my phone to text him.

"Hey, beautiful."

I looked up and found a pair of the most hypnotic eyes locked on mine. Still, I turned around to see if the woman he wanted was behind me. There was no one else there. When I turned back, his smirk deepened.

"Don't tell me your man doesn't compliment you?"

I followed his gaze to my ring. *He's hitting on me, even though he knows I'm married.* I shouldn't be surprised because it happened regularly. This was just the first time I was open for business, so to speak.

"Actually, he doesn't." In a move that shocked the two of us, I slipped my ring off and placed it in my bag.

The attractive stranger took the seat next to me. "Can I buy you a drink?"

"Sure."

We gave our orders to the bartender, and my shoulders relaxed.

Already, the stress from the hustle and bustle of the airport faded. Walter asked me what I wanted. I wanted simple conversations with handsome men who found me attractive. Was I justified in that desire?

"Are you coming or going?" he asked.

I was deep in thought with my mouth wide open. He reached over and gently closed it.

"I'm sorry. I don't mean to be forward. It was just distracting." He blushed. "I'm Rob... Is—is your husband here?"

My mouth hung open again. He went from flirtatious to spooked in a manner of moments. He stood abruptly and walked off.

"Hey, beautiful," Walter teased.

I slapped his arm. "What did you do? What was wrong with him?"

"You supposed to wait until we get to Florida, and he obviously wasn't about nothin' if he was intimidated by my mere presence." Walt's smile deepened.

Walter Dizzy Simmons was frightening when he didn't like someone. His size was enough to send anyone running. Walt's locs and build made him look like he was a defensive player for the McHaven Wolves.

"There you go looking fine again," he said with his lip curled up toward his nose.

I rolled my eyes. Chanté had bullied me into getting an outfit for every part of the trip, including my flights. She said I would not be one of those women dressed like a man in sweatpants and a bonnet. She agreed that I could wear leggings. I paired them with a pair of crisp white sneakers and a fitted white hoodie beneath a winter vest that both stopped above my ass.

Apparently, Chanté had done well based on the response from other men and Walter's grumpy mood.

"Hurry up and finish your baby drink so we can get on our plane," he fussed.

"Is this what my hall pass is going to be like? Are you vetting anyone who compliments me?"

He flinched. Walter had been acting weird all week. He must have really been worried about seeing Zanaé. I wasn't—at least not anymore. I sang and shouted my worries out on the car ride over. Either Zanaé and the client would like my idea, or they wouldn't.

Walt

MEN OGLED Bree from the time I saw her at the bar until we touched down in Florida and arrived at the *Carnelian*. To top it off, she hadn't worn that tiny starter ring Lance gave her. I couldn't figure out why the hell it bugged me so much.

Her glow up irked me almost as much as Lance did. At least with him, what I saw was what I got. These new men could be all types of foolishness. I'd barely noticed the provocative women at the resort until Bree addressed one of them.

"This is my coworker, sis, and he's super single."

The half-dressed woman high-fived Bree and gave me her best attempt at bedroom eyes. She handed me a card and told me to call her later. I nodded cordially and increased my pace to keep up with Brielle.

"What are you doing?" Bree asked when she saw me beside her at the reception desk.

"Checking in." I was flustered as shit.

"No. I mean she was hot. What's wrong with you?" Bree's curious eyes were on me.

The hell if I know!

"I had a long morning. I need a shower," I lied. It was new for me to withhold my truth from Bree. Ever since she said she was ready to mingle and changed up her style, I hadn't kept it real with her. "What time will Chanté and Chase get here?"

She shifted her body to fully face me. For the first time since I met her, I had to fight to keep my eyes above her neck where they belonged.

"What did I do?" she asked, crossing her arms in front of her chest. The movement only intensified my urge to stare at her titties.

"Huh?"

"Am I suddenly not good company? You sound like you can't

wait to get away from me." She huffed then leaned her body in and embraced me. She did that whenever I was in a foul mood, and normally, it worked. We'd hugged a million times, but never did my body respond like it did this time. I stepped back.

"You're acting weird." I tried to flip it on her to get some space.

She scrunched her nose up at me. "No, I'm not. Call me when you're out of this funk."

Bree turned her attention to the receptionist, who gave me a lingering once over. Normally, I would have wanted nothing more than to collect a bunch of numbers. I was on the rebound from Melina, and none of these women wanted anything more than a night of fun. *What the hell is my problem?*

Bree tossed the hotel key in my direction.

"Trouble in paradise?" Winter, the receptionist, asked with a wink.

"We're coworkers," Bree announced and switched her thick frame in the opposite direction with every man's eyes on her ass, including mine.

Fuck!

Bree

I WOULD HAVE a good time whether Walt wanted to hang out with me or not. Why would he whisk me away from the guy at the bar only to get here and make it clear he wanted to do his own thing. Walter fell into moods. I wasn't unaccustomed to his tendency to loath life among the optimistic, but today, he hurt my feelings. After everything I'd been through with Lance, I deserved to be chipper if I wanted to.

The Carnelian suite I was in had a contemporary layout that almost gave a masculine vibe with the dark colors and the sleek, modern accessories. I couldn't wait to turn on the firepit, although the weather here didn't exactly require it.

"Chase coming? Chase here?" I mocked as I unpacked my suitcase. I'd made sure our rooms weren't next to each other when the receptionist checked us in, and luckily, we weren't, but on the way to my room, I saw he wasn't far. I rolled my eyes and continued to lay out my new clothes.

The leopard print one-piece bathing suit Chanté forced me to buy was the sexiest thing I'd ever worn. I was thirty-five-years old, and I would show some skin if I damn well pleased. I took a quick shower and did my after-shower hygiene. I made sure to oil my legs to give them that extra shine. I'd been thick my entire life, but after I had London, my curves were on another level.

The lighting in the bathroom made my body look like I was ready for a photo shoot. The bikini wax Chanté insisted on had come in clutch for more than my potential hall pass. This bathing suit didn't leave much to the imagination. It completely covered my midsection but in a corset fashion. I was in decent shape—I just wasn't skinny.

My hips were exaggerated, and my substantial breasts were mostly exposed because of the low cut of the suit. The back gave just enough of a peek at my ass to let a man know there was heaven underneath it.

I giggled. When had I lost touch with my body? And who was this bad bitch in my mirror?

"Welcome back, sis," I said to myself as I applied light makeup to my face.

I was bullied for the large, round size of my lips when I was a child. Now that people paid good money for hips and lips like mine, it was much easier to embrace them. I added gloss over my red lip and gathered my beach bag. I sighed when I saw *A Naughty Rendezvous* tucked in my suitcase. *What the hell, why not?*

I tossed the book in with my cell and grabbed my hotel key, then headed for the pool. I didn't bother with a cover-up because I wanted to carry as little as I could get away with. If I got cold, I'd wear one of the resort robes. *Who gon' check me?*

The pool was breathtaking. What I loved most about the area was how the water featured a central island with a currently vacant bar, that fanned out to private islands for an exclusive VIP experience. None of it was in use at this early afternoon hour, but that didn't take away from the splendor.

It was barely noon. Maybe more guests would arrive later in the evening. For now, I would take advantage of the privacy.

The pool was positioned in the direction of the ocean and made it appear like we could fall into it if we got too close. The January weather in Florida was much warmer than McHaven this time of year. I couldn't wipe the smile from my face if I tried.

Walt

I TOOK a cold shower and still couldn't shake how fine Brielle was. There! I admitted I was attracted to my best friend. I had no idea what to do about it. We had so much history together that I couldn't imagine ruining it because I was a creep.

One makeover and I'd lost my mind. I'd also acted like a jerk. I was rude to her because I couldn't bear her free and floaty energy. I wanted her happy, but seeing it had kicked my libido up a notch in a way that was inappropriate for a friend. These were the times I wished I could call Mason, my mother's baby daddy. The conversation would inevitably lead to a fight, so it was out of the question.

I paced my suite in a towel. What if I said something dumb? What if I did something dumb? I rummaged through my pants for my cell.

ME:

Are y'all here?

CHANTÉ:

I literally just turned my phone on. We landed about five minutes ago. What's wrong?

ME:

I need you and Chase to hurry up so I can have a little more testosterone around me

CHANTÉ:

Aht aht! This ain't no bro kind of trip. This is a Chanté and Chase role play getaway

ME:

Ugh

CHANTÉ:

lol. I might call you when we get there, but
don't wait up.

Fuck!

I took a slow, deep breath and counted to ten. I grabbed my trunks and headed for the pool. At least there I could find an attractive woman to pass the time with. It had obviously been too long if I was obsessing over Brielle and her stacked body. The *Carnelian Resort and Spa* was a dream come true.

Had Joi not made the reservations, I doubted I would have tried to visit. The moment I stepped outside, I saw the smoothest hips and legs I'd ever seen. This woman lifted herself out of the pool like a scene from a movie, making my dick jump. I hadn't acted this horny since high school.

I strolled confidently in her direction and took a seat across from where she stood. I couldn't wait to see her face. With a body that captivating, she had to be a ten. She pulled her bathing suit from her ass, and I was jealous. I could've taken care of that for her. I chuckled to myself, which got her attention.

Shit! I should have known from the hair, but I was too preoccupied with her ass. Brielle waved and headed in my direction. *Fuck my life!*

"That water feels expensive." She gushed.

Seeing her up close was worse than the back of her. I'd seen Bree's body before. We'd visited the pool plenty of times, but I couldn't recall seeing her in so little clothes since she had her kid. London Bridges had done her body good! She lay back on one of the lounge chairs and I moaned.

"Walter Dizzy Simmons! Why are you acting strange? I swear you'd rather me be my normal mousy self. What's your problem?"

The scowl she wore was as sexy as her pouty lips.

"Uh, nah. I think I'm sick," I lied again.

"You got the bubble guts?" She smirked up at me. Unspeakable acts fluttered through my mind, and my body stiffened. I sat down awkwardly on the chair next to her. I was in trouble.

"You got jokes."

"Anyway, I'm worried about the hall pass." Her voice was soft, and it sent vibrations through my chest. I'd always wanted to protect Brielle, but now the reasons weren't only motivated by friendship. I would guard her heart, even if I had to protect her from me.

"Talk to me, girl."

Brielle Kari Barnes regarded me like I hung the stars. My pulse quickened, and my head was a jumbled mess. Her comfort was the only thing that kept me tuned in.

"What if I can't get somebody interested?" She dropped her eyes, and it did something to me.

I reached over and lifted her chin. "Are you serious? There's not a man who's seen you that hasn't fallen over himself staring and praying for a chance to get your attention."

Water filled her slanted eyes, and I had to force myself not to kiss her. *What the hell am I thinking?*

"You have to say that, Dizzy. You're my best friend."

What if I said fuck being friends? I shook my head, hopeful my irrational thoughts would clear. Bree mistook it as a response to her statement.

"You're not my friend?" Her voice was silky, and I swallowed hard.

Hell nah!

I nodded. "Bree, you're fine fine. I wasn't just gassing you when I saw this new hair of yours. Now you got your body ody ody out and you think you're gonna have a hard time finding a man? Girl, please."

She leaned up and in my direction. I stilled and my eyes closed of their own accord. When I opened them again, she was inches from my face. Brielle placed a sweet kiss on my cheek. "Thank you, Walter."

I shot to my feet with a towel strategically covering my dick. I was an almost forty-year-old man unable to control an erection induced by my favorite person in the world. "I'm a go lie down for a second."

"We don't have anything on the itinerary until Sunday afternoon. Call me tomorrow. Maybe we can hit the bar Saturday night and you can be my wingman."

My mouth went dry. "For sure," I said as I backed away from her and booked it to my room. My body was jittery as I walked inside the resort. How the hell would I survive this trip?

"Hey, Walter," Joi purred. She appeared out of nowhere. She was also dressed in a skimpy bathing suit and a cover-up that only highlighted her nakedness.

I still hadn't recovered from my discombobulated state after Bree's innocent kiss. Deep down, I wished she would have found my mouth. It was too much to process in such a short amount of time.

"Hey, boss," I muttered in a panic. I was clueless on any other way to address her. It was my way of reminding her of our professional dynamic.

"Joi, please. How was the pool?" Her eyes raked over my body.

"It was good, but I'm not feeling well, so I'm going to lie down."

She attempted to say more, but I turned on my heels and headed for the elevator.

Bree

Around seven o'clock Saturday evening, Chanté texted me that she and Chase had touched down yesterday but had been too preoccupied to link up. I was only a little envious of her role-playing plans with her husband. I loved that for her, but I also wanted it for me. Instead of letting myself fall down a rabbit hole of despair, I ordered room service.

My meal was exquisite. If I didn't plan to mingle at the bar, I would have preferred to experience that kind of food inside the restaurant. It had been months since I enjoyed a meal without little fingers tugging on me. My lip trembled. I missed my sonshine.

I texted Lance.

ME:
How is he?

Lance replied with a picture of London on his knees with a truck. He looked up just in time. When London wasn't happy, I could tell. His school sent me pictures throughout the day, even if he'd just finished crying. He was delighted to be with Lance. I saved the image right away.

ME:
Thank you

LANCE:

Of course. I got him. Try and enjoy yourself if you can

If he only knew. I wouldn't allow myself to put too much stock into Lance's new helpfulness. Why the hell did he want to be cooperative all of a sudden?

I showered in preparation for my mingling. My thoughts drifted back to Walter. He acted as though mingle was a curse word. He was supposed to be my wingman tonight, but I had no intention of begging him to be there for me. First, he would assure me that I was fine fine and didn't have anything to worry about, then he'd turn around and put an ocean of distance between us. *Grouchy ass man.* This whole scenario was out of character for me, but I was ready to try to get my own needs met like he and Chanté suggested.

I rolled my eyes until I saw my reflection in the mirror. *Yasss, bish!* By the time I was dressed, it was nine p.m. My fitted jeans hugged my curves like a second skin. The holes at my thighs and knees added an edge that was perfect for an evening at the bar. Chanté swore the black leotard wasn't too much, especially since I brought an unbuttoned black jacket to wear over it.

I wore a pair of black open-toe stiletto sandals that would require me to walk carefully and slip out of them after a few drinks, but they made my ass sit perfectly. My pedicure was flawless, and I was beat from head to toe. Why hadn't I done this sooner? I was more aligned now than when I was miserably holding out for a loveless marriage.

I sat on the bed and closed my eyes. *God, I have no idea what I'm doing. Keep me safe, and if I'm really wilin out and going too far, help me to find contentment enjoying my own company this weekend. Thank you for this trip. Thank you for London. Thank you for my friends.*

A weight lifted off my shoulders. Tonight was the night I would shoot my shot. God willing, a mouthwatering man would bring me out of my drought in a most unforgettable way. Without a doubt, I was justified!

seven

Walt

I SAT AT THE BAR ALONE AND SEXUALLY FRUSTRATED. Several women approached me, but I sent them all away. My head was so twisted up over Brielle I couldn't entertain them. She had asked if I would be her wingman tonight, but after I saw her in her bathing suit yesterday, I doubted I could be near her without doing something I might regret.

I nursed whatever dark liquor the bartender gave me. I'd barely spoken to her when I sat down. Instead, I just gave her a nod. She was cute and she was a hustler. She took one look at me, returned my nod, then slid whatever was in my glass toward me with a wink. I would leave her a big ass tip because, thanks to her, my body finally relaxed.

My eyes were locked on the view outdoors. The floor-to-ceiling windows facing the ocean calmed me. Or maybe it was the strategically placed neon purple lighting. The weather was amazing, and it was truly a relief not to have to wear a coat like back home.

A guy who'd been in my area—nursing the same drink for the last hour—bolted from his chair with a "hell yeah." When I found the inspiration for his swear, I almost blacked out. My legs went numb, and my eyes bucked. Brielle was dressed in an outfit that was straight out of a wet dream. It took all the restraint I could muster to remain planted in my chair.

I had no right to suggest she take a hall pass then try to intervene. The man hadn't stepped out of line, so I would hang back. Whatever he said made her blush. Brielle was stunning. Her hair and her personality were unmatched.

The man ordered Bree a drink while I did my best to blend into the background. The bar was big enough that I would have to go out of my way to make my presence known since he had her full attention.

Twenty painful minutes crept by with Bree and this stranger engaged in a private conversation accented by various drinks served to her by the bartender. At one point, she let him drink from her glass. My heart hadn't slowed since she arrived, but I'd been on my best behavior until he stood. When Brielle lifted from her seat and stumbled, I was at her side in seconds.

"Can I help you?" the nameless man asked.

My watchful eyes were locked on Bree's.

"Don't worry, Lamar, it's just my babysitter," she said. Her eyebrows were bunched together, and she wore a frown on her stunning face as she glared at me. "I'm not drunk, Walt. It's my heels."

I peered down at them, and my throat went dry. I thought the heels she wore to the office were sexy, but these showcased her pretty toes, making me fantasize about putting them in my mouth. I scanned her body from her feet and back up her curvy frame to her face. Her makeup made me want to lick her everywhere, and whatever perfume she wore had me dizzy.

"Who is this, Bree?"

My fists were balled, and my jaw clenched. "I'm her date," I lied before I could stop myself.

"Walter!" Bree squealed.

"I had a good time, but I'm not looking for any drama. It was nice meeting you, Brielle."

He went in for a hug, but I pulled Bree's plush body close. Lamar threw his hands up and walked off.

"What is your problem, Walter?" Bree asked with a flush across her light brown cheeks. "This is the second man you've chased away from me, even though I'm not who you want to spend your vacation with. One minute, I'm too sad and I need to put myself first. The next minute, I'm too free with my body, then you act like it's a crime for me to say I want to mingle."

She pushed her finger in my chest. She was right about everything, but all I could think about was kissing her, so that was exactly what I did. I leaned down and used my mouth to communicate what I couldn't do with words. I wanted Brielle for myself. *I* wanted her body, and *I* wanted to be the man she cashed in her hall pass for.

I held her jaw with my hand and used my tongue to wet her cherry-flavored lips. Her soft moans egged me on, so I returned my lips to hers once again. We kissed for long moments until she pulled away. Bree gazed up at me, and for the life of me, I couldn't tell whether she liked or regretted what I'd done.

I'd violated our friendship in a way that couldn't be ignored. She'd be well within her rights to slap me.

"What—What was that?" she asked.

I ran my hand through my locs. I'd fucked things up with

Brielle. "I'm sorry. You just look good enough to eat. I don't know what came—"

Either I hallucinated or Bree leaned up and kissed me back. Her full red lips against mine were evidence that this was real—I hadn't imagined it. My body stiffened, and she was close enough to feel it too.

She pulled back and peered around her. "I think we should—"

"We can stop. I couldn't help myself," I admitted, stuffing my hands into my pockets.

She gave me a smirk that made my heart stutter. My pants tightened. "I was going to say we should go to my room. One of our coworkers might see us."

My eyebrows flew up. "For real?"

She nodded. Brielle grabbed my hand and led me to the elevators toward our rooms. I almost fell a couple times because I was so preoccupied with her ass that I hadn't bothered to watch my step. She peered at me with her bottom lip tucked between her teeth. I rested my hand on her lower back as we waited for the elevator. Could she hear my heartbeat through my chest?

When the elevator doors closed, she attacked me in the most welcomed way. It had been over a year since she had sex. Her lips connected with mine hungrily. I didn't try to suppress the groans that morphed into growls when she twirled her tongue in my mouth. Her husband was a damn fool. The elevator dinged, but we kept at it until she lost her balance.

We stopped and burst into laughter. She was my friend, and so far, that hadn't changed; only now we'd added sexual chemistry to our dynamic. I held the elevator open, then quickly decided to hell with letting her remove her heels. I couldn't wait. I picked Brielle up and tossed her over my shoulder.

She giggled. I hustled to her door, biting her ass on the way. I returned her to her feet so she could unlock her suite. She didn't say anything. Bree stood and stared at me for several minutes. *Damn, she's fine.*

Once we were inside, I leaned and kissed her passionately. The smell of apricots intensified since she'd sprayed her perfume in the enclosed space. When we needed to catch our breaths, I separated from her lips then latched on to her neck.

"Walter."

"Yeah, Bree Bree?" I asked between licks. I used my tongue to lick underneath her chin and back to her neck. I trailed kisses there until I was at the base of her ear.

"Let me go and change."

"OK." I wanted to say hell no, but I also didn't want to push my luck. I was down for whatever Brielle was comfortable with.

I parked my body on the extended couch in her suite. The open concept mirrored mine, but she'd somehow transformed hers and given it a feminine touch. I steadied my breathing and let my eyes scan her space. There were outfits laid out beside me. Each of them was sexier than anything I'd ever seen Bree wear. Chanté didn't lie when she said she would be fine as fuck.

Brielle sauntered out of the bathroom, and my mouth fell open. The gold color of the symmetrical designed one piece made my dick throb. It was like her bathing suit, only lacey and a hell of a lot more revealing.

I had to wipe my face because I drooled. Brielle was orgasmic in the skimpy lingerie she wore. I couldn't believe she almost shared this with someone else. I stood and strolled in her direction. This would be the best sex of her life, or I would die trying.

The confidence she had at the bar was replaced with hesitation. She may not have known why I'd been such a jerk this past week, but I could read Bree like the back of my hand. Her usual timid nature around all things sexual had returned. Her eyes fell from mine, and she gasped when they landed between my legs. I was fully erect and hadn't tried to hide it.

"We don't have to."

"You don't want to?" she asked in a hushed tone. Her eyes were on mine once again.

I looked down at my dick. "We both know I do, but not until you're comfortable."

Her shoulders sagged. "I shouldn't be surprised that I'm chickening out. At least with you, I'm not as embarrassed. Lamar might not have been so understanding."

"Man, fuck... forget him. I'm here and I want you. We can go slow if that's what you need; just let me be your hall pass, Brielle," I practically begged.

"OK," she whispered.

I let my eyes rake across the exposed parts of her body I'd never had the pleasure of seeing. Bree still hadn't relaxed. I grabbed her hand and led her to the couch I'd abandoned to see her up close. I sat and motioned for her to sit on the opposite side away from me. When I patted my lap, her lips curled into a mischievous smile.

I rubbed her feet like I always did when she was frazzled, but this time, her body didn't just relax... it responded. Bree's nipples hardened beneath the fabric covering her breasts. Her lips parted, and the fire I saw at the bar had returned. I rubbed her legs, then moved from the couch and directed her to lie face down so I could rub her back. I kneaded her shoulders and planted kisses on the velvety skin of her backside.

Her cheeks were phenomenal. Everything in me wanted to slap them, but that would have to come later.

"How about the 'can I' game?"

"What's that?" she asked with her head propped up on her hands.

"Before I touch you sexually, I'll ask permission."

"I'm good with that."

She shifted to her side to face me.

"Can I touch you here?" I asked as I pointed to the curve of her round ass.

She nodded.

I ran my hands across her yams and smiled when she moaned. Her man was an idiot. With a yamborghini like the one Bree had, I doubted I would ever let her up for air.

"Can I touch you here?" I asked as I pointed at her lips.

She nodded again, and I ran my fingers across her sinfully full lips. When I moved my hand, she wet them, and my dick bounced.

"Can I touch you here?" I asked as I pointed to her titty.

"Yes, Walter."

I palmed her breast and used my thumb to caress her already hardened nipple.

"I wanna put it in my mouth," I admitted.

Her eyes sprang open. "You don't have to ask anymore."

I pulled her nipple into my mouth through the lace material. She arched her body toward me, and I held her tightly in place. I used my left hand to push aside the flimsy material that covered the sensitive area between her legs. She was already wet.

"Damn, Brielle," I whined. My thumb rubbed tight circles against her clit, and her legs shook. I moved my head from her breasts because I needed to see her face enjoying my hand.

It was contorted, and her lips were tucked in her mouth. I wasn't sure what came over me, but I reached down and ripped the lingerie. She said I didn't have to ask. I wanted to taste her so bad my tongue twitched. I shifted her so her legs faced me instead of the other end of the couch.

She yelped and watched me expectantly. I dove in face first and slurped on her pussy like she was the best soup I'd ever eaten. Her moans grew louder, but I wouldn't let up. I would please Brielle until she begged me to stop. I liked eating pussy and often had my head pushed away because women swore it was too intoxicating.

Brielle deserved good head and good dick, and it was an honor to be the one to give it to her. I pulled her clit into my mouth and sucked on it lightly, then I increased the pressure. She wound her hips where she sat, then clamped her soft thighs against my head. I glanced up at her and saw her hands brush by her breasts like she wanted stimulation there too. I freed her breasts then placed her hands on them for her.

In no time, she squeezed her own nipples. Bree had gotten comfortable with me, despite her initial hesitation.

"Walter," she moaned.

Sensations of pleasure washed over me, and all I'd done was put my hands and mouth on her. I was in trouble when she returned the favor. Bree's head fell back as her entire body vibrated. I barely blinked as I watched her unravel before me. *I love this woman. I love her more than I already have for the past fifteen years. I love love her.*

What the fuck did I do?

Bree

I'M GOING TO HELL. My body responded to Walter in a way I'd never experienced before him. I wasn't a virgin when I married Lance, but I'd practiced celibacy for the most part. An energy that had been dormant in me awakened the moment Walt's lips connected with mine.

His frustration with me was sexual. He'd been an ass ever since I changed my hair, and I said I was ready to mingle. It all made sense now.

I couldn't do much of an introspective deep dive, because as my body came down from a powerful orgasm, I was lifted from the couch and walked to the bed positioned in the center of my suite. If I wanted to change my mind, I needed to speak now or forever hold my peace. My elbows rested on his solid shoulders until I was gently laid on the bed.

Dizzy was my best friend. In all the time I'd known him, we'd kept it platonic. I had a dream about him once, but I didn't put too much stock into it. It was a harmless fantasy, because both of us had partners, and I would never have acted on those lewd desires from my subconscious. What would happen to our friendship after a night of passion?

Walt stood and stared down at me. It was a bad idea to compare him with my soon-to-be ex, but I'd never been on the verge of an orgasm from Lance's eyes alone. Now that I was practically naked, my inhibitions were down, and I could see Walter for who he was. Beyond a thoughtful, cranky human being, he was captivating. His hooded eyes sat lower than normal, and his locs hung around his shoulders untamed.

"I can satisfy you better than that if you let me." His hands were behind his back as if it was the only way for him to keep them off me. He surveyed my wide frame and had a wordless, lurid conversation with me that caused aftershocks to reverberate through my being.

I lifted from my elbows. I had an inexplicable desire to have Walter in my mouth. I had been pent up for months upon months, and besides the smutty books I read and the use of my own hand, I had no other release. I yanked at his pants as he sucked in a breath.

I freed him and stared at the masterpiece between his legs. *Holy shit! Walter Simmons is blessed.* No wonder why he walked and spoke the way he did. With a dick like his, he had absolutely nothing to prove. Melina had played her cards wrong to let this python slip between her fingers.

I wet my lips. The moment I put my mouth on Walter, I was hooked. His hand automatically went to the back of my curly afro. It made my center thump that although Walt had been patient with me, he still didn't treat me like glass. In many ways, I was a walking contradiction. I had been raised sexually repressed, so I'd probably never be comfortable with random conversations about sex. On the other hand, I'd been deprived of my primal urges by the person who was supposed to allow me the space and safety to indulge. My body yearned to play, and Dizzy was more than willing to engage.

As if we'd done this a million times before, I opened wide and accepted his full length as he guided my head toward him. I hummed, and he reacted to the vibrations. I held his girth in one hand while I worked and clamped my fingers from my free hand around my left thumb.

One of the *Brown Baddies* books detailed how a particular female character gave the best head when she applied pressure to her left thumb. It helped her with her gag reflex. It didn't help me, but it certainly gave me confidence. I choked on Walter's length until my eyes watered, but neither of us stopped.

"Shit!" he spat. "If your mouth feels this good, I can't imagine what your pussy feel like."

I slurped while I exaggerated the sound, then reluctantly pulled away. I needed this man inside of me now. I stood from the bed and removed what was left of my lingerie. Lust and another emotion I couldn't put my finger on clouded Walter's eyes. He turned and grabbed for his pants. When he did, I saw the sexiest ass I'd ever seen.

He sheathed himself and lifted me. He didn't even break a sweat, and I wasn't light by any means. Without another word, Walter entered me while we stood at the edge of the bed. I came the moment he was fully nestled inside of me. It was my second orgasm of the night, but my first dick induced one in over a year.

I finally understood what those women raved about in the pages of my favorite books. Before tonight, I thought multiple orgasms was a myth. Walter slammed into me as his mouth latched onto my neck. With my arms wrapped tightly around him, I held on for dear life. He leaned back so we were face to face.

Our earlier wordless conversation made perfect sense. He desperately wanted to be inside of me. Now that we were joined in the most intimate way, I couldn't decipher what else he needed to say.

"Just tell me," I said through ragged breaths.

He stopped and knelt on the bed. He shifted us effortlessly so that I was on my back, and he was on top of me. He kissed me to avoid my question, and I didn't have the willpower to point it out. Walter rocked in and out of me, making my body experience a myriad of sensations. He wasn't gentle, but he also wasn't too rough. He was the perfect mixture of patient and X-rated.

I almost let another idiot be my hall pass.

"Turn over, baby," he commanded.

I didn't think twice before my ass was tooted in Walter's

direction. A low growl rumbled in his throat. Part of me wanted him to take it easy, but another part of me wouldn't mind if he lost control. I was sure I could handle him. I craned my neck to see his eyes watching me appreciatively.

"Put your hands on the headboard, Brielle."

I moaned and promptly followed his instructions. My back arched dramatically, and the fabric of the comforter brushed against my already sensitive nipples. His hands wrapped around my hips.

"You ready for me?"

I was afraid if I answered him, I would orgasm again and black out. I wanted to be present for whatever was coming next. When I didn't respond, he took both his hands and clapped my cheeks. The pain was brief and enjoyable. I turned my head to find a smirk on his handsome face.

"I like it," I said with a smirk of my own. He smacked my ass again while I watched. "You just gonna smack me, or you gonna fuck me?"

His eyebrows flew up. "Brielle, what's gotten into you?"

"Hopefully you," I retorted.

With one last slap, he brought his body closer to mine. "I've wanted to do that since you stepped into my office with your new hair and clothes."

I stole another glance at him. "Why didn't you say anything?"

He lined himself up with my treasure and entered me fiercely. "I didn't know how," he said in a strained voice.

Walter fucked me like I deserved. I forgot what question I asked and what day it was. All I could focus on was how good his balls felt as they smacked my ass with each of his movements. I reached between my legs and stroked them. Walter's pace and intensity increased.

"Fuck!"

He didn't slow down until he met his peak, and that third orgasm I worried about exploded inside of me. I collapsed onto the bed and was pulled to my side. Walter held me snugly against him. His warmth and the multiple climaxes sent me into the deepest sleep I'd had in a long time.

Walt

"Where you going, Bree?" I asked as I blinked into the darkness of her hotel room. I could barely see, but I missed her presence the moment she stirred.

When she didn't respond, I continued. "Don't regret me tonight, please. I'll leave first thing in the morning; just stay in bed with me now. I'll beg if I have to." My voice was strained, although I tried to conceal it. Hopefully, she would only recognize the heavy sound of sleep surrounding each of my words.

"I just need the bathroom, Walter." When she leaned in and kissed my lips, I was instantly hard. Bree giggled when she saw my dick jump.

I lay with my hands resting behind my head, unwilling to allow panic to set in. I'd had the most satisfying night of my life with my very best friend. Brielle was everything I wanted in a woman. She was a devoted mother with a kind soul. It didn't hurt that she laughed at all my jokes and was already comfortable with me in a way she likely hadn't been with other men.

If I fucked up the easy nature of our relationship because I insisted on being her hall pass, I'd never forgive myself. She finished her business in the bathroom and stood at the door. Neither of us bothered to put on clothes at any point during the night. Her silhouette made my already eager dick harder. With her lips between her teeth and her eyes trained on my body, she sauntered across the room.

"We should probably talk at some point," she said as she climbed back into bed with me.

"I promise we will... right after you ride me." I hadn't moved my hands from behind my head, and Bree hadn't lifted her eyes from between my legs. I motioned for her to come closer. "Don't act shy now. The way you took it last night..." I closed my eyes at the memory.

Bree inched in my direction, and it was all I needed to grasp her body and pull her even closer. She straddled me, and I barely had to guide myself into her because she was so damn wet. She sank down on me, and for the first time since I was a teenager, I had to concentrate to avoid finishing early.

My head was a mess. My entire outlook on love shifted. Brielle had me considering marriage. *What the hell is wrong with you, Dizzy?* Her moans pulled me out of my internal battle. My eyes sprang open to find her head flung back. She arched her titties in my direction, and I wasted no time leaning up and pulling them between my lips.

I rubbed my hands down the delicate skin of her back. If there was only a way to make this moment last forever. Her thighs resting on my lap was pure heaven. Nothing was better than this. I grasped her ass and watched as she had another Walter induced orgasm.

I pulled her closer and latched onto her neck. This time, I didn't care if I left bite marks behind. She was mine. Would Bree agree to that? With every fiber of my being, I wanted her as my best friend and lover.

She moved her face to meet mine then shoved her tongue in my mouth. It was my undoing.

"Damn, Bree." I grunted as I held her hips and rocked inside of her a final time. I fell back onto the bed and accepted her weight when she followed suit. We both drifted off to sleep with our bodies still connected.

I AWOKE to Bree's whimpers. She sniffed and tried to keep quiet so she wouldn't wake me. She was still in my arms with her back to me. I willed my body not to respond to her soft cheeks, but my dick had a mind of its own.

"You're up," she said sarcastically.

Sunrays poked between the edges of the wall-to-ceiling curtains. It was Sunday morning, but I hadn't bothered to check the time. My alarm was set to alert me when I needed to dress for our presentation.

I turned Bree so I could see her face. Once again, she stole the breath from my lungs. Had she gotten prettier? Brielle Kari Barnes was glowing, and I had a hunch she didn't want to.

I'd been around when Bree cried on more occasions than I could count. In the beginning, her weeping was a result of her overbearing and demanding family. Later, she'd burst into tears over her poor excuse for a husband. Now, I was positive her wet face was because of me.

I opened my mouth, but no words came out.

I finally settled on, "What can I do?"

She gave me a weak smile. "You've done plenty, Walter."

"Yeah, but do you regret it? Do you regret me?" There was no way she missed the pain in my tone this time. I was powerless to hide it. I'd put her in an unfair situation, but Lance would have to rip her from my cold, dead hands before I would willingly allow her to lower herself to his level ever again.

Her eyes fell, and my heart squeezed in my chest.

"Last night—last night was the best night of my life. I've never been so satisfied. That's why you and Chanté pushed me to do it, right?"

I nodded. I held my breath because if there was a 'but,' I wouldn't survive.

"How are we supposed to do the presentation together?" Her eyes were wide with concern.

I fell out in laughter. I'd had a soft spot for this woman for years, and this was why. I had convinced myself that she was about to kick my black ass out of her room because of what we'd done, but all she was worried about was work.

"I thought you wanted to talk about last night?" I pressed.

"I am talking about it. I doubt I can pretend I haven't seen you naked." Her eyes raked over my exposed chest. Most of my tattoos were strategically etched into places on my skin so that they could be covered when I was dressed. Women liked them, and apparently, good girl Brielle did too.

I smiled brightly in response to her concerns because I wasn't hearing a problem. It faltered when I saw trepidation clouding her slanted eyes.

"We're going to be in a room with Joi and Zanaé later this afternoon. It's not going to go well if you keep looking at me like that."

"Huh?" She'd caught me with my eyes on her titties.

"You're gonna have clothes on, I hope. Be for real. You can't expect me not to stare at these masterpieces." I leaned in and pulled her nipple into my mouth. When she didn't stop me, I eased on top of her and between her legs.

"You want me to stop fuckin' you, Bree?" I growled as I rested my dick at the entryway to my new heaven.

"You're still my hall pass, right?" she moaned.

"Hell yeah."

I dove in, and each time I entered her, I swear I fell harder. I couldn't tell whether I was whipped or my feelings for Bree ran deeper than lovers and friends. Relief washed over me when she'd only expressed concerns about work. I had no idea what I'd do if I let my desire to be the one to please her cost me our friendship. So far, she hadn't mentioned her soon-to-be ex man, and I couldn't be happier.

She had her thick thighs wrapped around my waist. In the recesses of my mind, I tried to determine if they felt better there or clamped around my head. I was Dizzy alright. Brielle's pussy had that effect on me.

Fuck work. I'd completely forgotten about Zanaé, who I could've convinced to spend an evening with me. Now that I had Bree, I wasn't interested.

I was deep in her walls, and I hadn't let up, even when her moan hit a soprano octave. Her nails dug into the skin of my back, but those sensations only served to egg me on.

"Don't run from this dick, Bree." I lifted her legs and rested them on my shoulders. "Take it like a good girl."

Her back arched, and her eyes rolled to the back of her head. Bree's mouth was wide open, and memories flitted through my mind of how easily she'd taken me deep in her throat. I was surprised as hell that Bree let me pull the back of her head while she sucked my dick. Melina never let me do that shit. My toes curled, but I continued my measured strokes.

I wanted to stay in Brielle's pussy until the sun set and rose again.

"Walter!"

Her entire body vibrated. She shook while her slanted eyes found mine. It was too much. The fact that I'd provided her more pleasure in a day than she'd had in the past year was my undoing. I plunged into her three more times as she rode out her own orgasm. When she lifted, grabbed my head between her hands, and kissed me hungrily, I released the biggest nut of my life.

"Shit, girl!"

She wiped the perspiration from my brow and regarded me curiously.

"What?" I asked.

Bree wanted to talk. Something was always cooking in that big brain of hers. If it wasn't that we had to stop fucking or related to Lance, she could talk to me about anything.

I rolled to the side, and we separated, but I quickly pulled her ass snugly against the front of my wet dick.

"I like this too much," she whispered.

"Hogwash!"

She craned her neck to look back at me while she giggled. My eyes were closed because I'd put in work. I gave this woman everything I had and probably needed electrolytes to avoid dehydration.

"I'm serious. I'm going to hell." Her voice was softer and no longer playful.

"Don't say no shit like that." *Fuck, I just want to sleep with her thick body on mine.* She rolled on her back, and I propped myself up to give her my full attention. Tired or not, I would've done anything for this woman.

"I should have left him first."

My eyebrows flew up.

There were a million unanswered questions in her beautiful eyes, but still she looked away.

"I... You want to leave him?"

"I have for a while, but I was afraid there wasn't anything better."

"Am I better?" I shouldn't have asked her, but I needed to know the answer, even at the risk of the ultimate rejection.

She nodded.

"You're not worried about our friendship?"

Her head flew in my direction. "Are you?" she asked. Panic covered her face along with her untamed afro.

I swept curls away from her cheek and rubbed it. *This has got to be a dream.* "I don't know about you, but there isn't another person I'd rather do this with than you." I cleared my throat. I hadn't meant to admit that. Bree had always been so easy to talk to. She was married but only on paper. Her ex and how she would untangle herself from him was my only concern.

Her wide smile returned. "Not even Zanaé?"

I scrunched my face and lifted my head as though I wasn't sure. I laughed when she pushed me in the chest. "That's different. I've had a crush on her for a long ass time."

There was a challenge in her eyes as she glared at me and shrugged her shoulders.

"I'm playing. I won't even look at her," I teased.

"You better. This presentation could mean big things for M3 and us. Besides, if you want Zanaé, I'm sure Lamar or Rob would be up for some fun."

My jaw clenched. She was messing with me, but I still didn't like that shit. It was bad enough that her child's father was in the picture. The last thing I wanted to think about was how another man was sniffing around what I knew was the best pussy this side of the Mississippi.

She stretched her body, and I tried not to be a creep. I couldn't keep my eyes off her.

"I must have really put it on you," Bree teased. She stood while I tracked her every movement. Brielle's body was magnificent. I wanted a wax sculpture of it in every room of my house. *Damn, I'm thirsty.*

"Why you say that?"

She turned around and bent over to pick up her robe. I moaned because shit!

"I've never known you to be a territorial man."

I sat up and scooted to the edge of the bed. The alarm on my phone chimed, and I was both annoyed and relieved. I wasn't ready for her to reject me, because I would absolutely try to fuck her again if she kept bending her body in front of me.

"That's because you're different."

She turned around and mounted me.

"Don't start. You heard my alarm," I said, even though my hands automatically wrapped around her ass.

"We could do a quickie," she said as she kissed the side of my neck. My dick sprang to attention just as her phone rang.

She got up, and I took the opportunity to dress while she answered. Part of me couldn't handle hearing a conversation between her and Lance.

"Hey, girl! How was your night?"

My shoulders relaxed. It was Chanté. I could tell by the way Bree's voice changed.

"You and Chase are some filthy freaks."

Once I was fully clothed, I nodded my head toward the door. She waved me off with a blush on her cheeks. Would she tell

Chanté about us? I slapped her ass loud enough to echo through the phone.

"See you soon," I said as I opened and closed the door behind me.

Bree quickly said, "That was the TV."

Chanté wouldn't fall for it because Brielle was a horrible liar.

Bree

THE CONFERENCE ROOM in the *Carnelian* was the most decadent workspace I'd ever had the pleasure of doing business in. The nearly seventeen-foot authentic oak table, in the center of the room, made our client and their celebrity brand ambassador look like we were discussing a million-dollar idea. My tangerine-colored bodycon dress hugged my frame in a way that was still classy because of the midi length. The twist front, one-shoulder design oozed boss babe. I silently thanked God that I allowed Chanté to have her way with my wardrobe; otherwise, my imposter syndrome would've had me in a chokehold the entire presentation.

Generally, I was a wreck in this type of work situation. I had no problem with the planning, but I struggled with execution. That was why Walter and I were such a great team. He kept me grounded and boosted my confidence when I got in my head.

Today was different. My idea would make everyone in this room a boatload of money, including the mega popstar seated a few feet away from me. Zanaé was stunning. Most of her face was covered with an expensive pair of oversized glasses, but her aura shone through. Her time was limited, so once we were set up, I jumped right in.

"*CocoaKiss Cosmetics* has an almost identical target audience as Zanaé's core fans."

I looked at Walt who hadn't moved his fine body nor had he managed to shift his eyes from mine. He was supposed to pull up the graph with the visual representation of the intersection between the two populations. I cleared my throat.

"Oh yeah," he mumbled. He turned and knocked his water bottle off the desk.

Zanaé's publicist pursed his lips. His skincare routine had his skin sparkling, but his patience was thin. If he pulled Zanaé away from this meeting, we'd never get another opportunity.

"It's just a little jetlag," I joked. I smiled at Walter whose face was uncharacteristically ghosted. I prayed I wasn't the reason he was off his game. We could figure out what we were *after* we secured this bag.

She laughed, so I continued.

"Let's cut to the chase, because I could show you the numbers anytime," I said as I nodded in Walter's direction. He had yet to regain his composure.

"I know you wear the product, but you and *CocoaKisses* have yet to do an official campaign together. I'm picturing a commercial featuring you in the studio with a small snippet of whatever new music you're about to drop playing in the background. You stop the engineer just before it gives away too much of the track and apply the lip gloss. You say to yourself 'when I look sexy, I sound sexy'."

An eerie silence fell across the room. Zanaé's ginormous bodyguard released an audible, "Hmph."

She swirled her chair around to face him. "You like that, Goliath?"

"Sounds like something you and Ant already say in real life," he added flatly.

Anton had his face between two electronic devices. "When she looks sexy, she *does* sound sexy." He rolled his eyes and resumed his work, clacking on both screens feverishly.

Zanaé removed her glasses. "Was this your idea?"

"Mine and his," I divulged.

When I found Walter's eyes were still glued to my ass, my center pulsed inappropriately. Unlike him, I remained poised on the outside. Zanaé gave him an unhurried once over. He finally tore his eyes from my body and gave her a small wave.

"Joi, send me the paperwork. We can shoot it here if your team is ready," Zanaé added.

When she stood, Goliath was at her side in a split second. How was someone that wide so fast? Anton closed his devices and tucked them neatly inside of a leather satchel. He was stylish, and although his features were delicate, he was not to be played with.

She walked over to where Walter and I stood. I motioned for him to join me. He hadn't said more than two words since Joi introduced us.

"You're going to make me a lot of money with this. I can feel it." She gushed as she took my hand.

"Thank you. I'm a huge fan of your work and your business endeavors. It's an honor to hear that from you."

She leaned in and asked, "How long have y'all been—"

"They're just friends," Joi cut in, oblivious to the change in my relationship with Walter.

Anton and Zanaé wore matching faces that called bullshit. Walter didn't help the situation with the goofy look he had plastered across his face.

"Good luck with that," Anton said as he and Goliath whisked Zanaé away.

"I'll be in touch with you two tomorrow," Joi said to us as she also left the conference room with a few other M3 employees.

"What the hell was that, Walter? Why did you pick today of all days to be mute?" I asked with my fists resting on my hips.

After what felt like an eternity, he flashed me an indecent smile. I tried to stay mad at him, but he was so damn fine in his business casual attire. His locs were pulled back neatly, although nothing else about him was tamed. Walter's hair was like a lion's mane, and it had caught the attention of Zanaé and her publicist. I returned his smile, despite my best efforts.

"Honestly, I was trying my best not to lift your dress and fuck you while all these people were still here."

My breath hitched. He had a filthy mouth, but it had never been directed at me before. Maybe I shouldn't be comfortable with the quick shift in our dynamic, but I was. I enjoyed the way his words swam from my ears and settled between my legs the same way he had a few hours earlier.

"And have you seen the way this outfit showcases these yams?" He closed the distance between us and lifted my hand to twirl me around for a three-sixty view, then whistled.

"Really, Dizzy?"

"Yes, dammit! You make my head dizzy. If you wasn't fine as frog hair, I could have helped or at least flirted with Zanaé. Shit, I barely looked at her."

"I noticed."

Despite the opened doors, he pulled me closer and grabbed a handful of my ass. Neither of us could keep our cool, nor could Walter keep his body off me. I'd been starved for attention for too long to protest. He found the side of my neck.

"You already left a mark," I moaned.

"Good. Maybe Lamar will keep his eyes off."

Is he really jealous over a man I spoke to for two seconds? I found his eyes, and he found my mouth. It was a pattern of his—in the past twenty-four hours—to kiss my questions away. I'd give him an out while we were busy with our work sexcation, but eventually, he would have to talk to me.

"How did the meeting go..."

Walter released me and stepped back, but the damage had already been done. A bewildered Aiden stood at the door. He'd seen me in Walter's arms. The cat was out of the bag. There went my justification.

nine

Walt

Bree had lost her earlier confidence, but I regained mine. I stood with my hands clasped in front of me, waiting for Aiden to say something stupid. He didn't. He cowered away just as I suspected he would. Brielle, on the other hand, had turned shaken by our being caught with my hands in her cookie jar.

"Bree—"

"I'm not…" She took a deep, steady breath.

She peered in my direction with tears crowding her eyes, and I wanted nothing more than to snap Aiden's intrusive neck. I pulled Brielle into me because I needed her close and hoped my proximity would ease her discomfort.

"I don't regret anything we've done together, Walter."

I blew out a breath. My heart couldn't handle it if she did. "What can I do?"

"Like I said this morning, you've done enough already." She flashed me a weak smile.

"I'm serious. Do you need me to dial it back in public? I'll do whatever you want." I released her. I stuffed my hands in my pockets and waited patiently for her to speak.

Her lips perked up. "First, I'll say why I'm upset, then I'll tell you what I need you to do."

My dick jumped. I pulled one of her curls to distract myself from what I hoped would be a freaky request on her part.

"Aiden represents the reality that awaits me once I leave this oasis. I miss London more than anything in the world, but to be with him, I have to face his father."

"I know, baby," fell out of my mouth. We hadn't determined what we were, but given the circumstances, it was natural for me to refer to her in that way while consoling her.

She tucked her juicy bottom lip between her teeth. I calculated the likelihood that she would let me fuck her in public after we'd just been caught then quickly dismissed the idea.

With her brows furrowed, she asked, "Do you want to be a father, Walter?"

That came out of nowhere. Her question hit me like a ton of bricks. I wanted to say that I didn't know, but I had the good sense not to.

"I love London Bridges. He is hands down the coolest kid I've ever met." I tugged at my tie. "But it's not like I had a great example of what a good dad is."

Her eyes dropped and my heart went with it. I was fucking up, and we hadn't even gotten started. I tilted her chin up. If she was asking me to be in her and London's life more permanently, then the answer was a hell yes. "I'm willing to learn."

"You don't have to say that."

"Bree, are you asking me to be around your kid?"

"Yes."

I lifted her from her feet and rested her soft cheeks on my forearm. "I'm not just your hall pass?"

Her upturned nose was scrunched. "Hmmm. Let's see how the rest of the trip goes."

I returned Brielle to the floor and kissed her like my life depended on it. When the need to breathe outweighed our moment of passion, she pulled back.

"I'm still worried about our jobs."

My face was in her neck when I added, "Fuck that job."

"I'm being for real. Joi is going to flip. She's never believed we were just friends, and she has a thing for you."

Once again, I reeled myself in and released her. She smelled like passion fruit, and I couldn't get enough. I cleared my throat and did my best to concentrate on her words and not her body. *Shit!*

"I don't want Joi."

She smiled at me innocently, and I winked in response.

"Come to my place," I pressed.

"Right now?"

I nodded. "Let me help you relieve some of this stress."

Her eyes bulged.

"Not that, nasty. I meant I could rub your feet while you read one of those trashy books."

"What if I *want* you to be nasty so I don't need those books?" She ran her hand down the center of my chest and retrieved her belongings from the conference table.

A growl rumbled in my throat. I came on this trip salty that Bree was ready to mingle; now I was on the receiving end of her giving mood. Nothing could snatch the goofy grin from my face.

We kept our hands to ourselves as we awaited the elevator. Other guests buzzed around us. Every now and then, I'd catch her staring up at me, biting her lip. When the elevator closed, she fidgeted beside me.

"What's wrong?" I whispered.

She pursed her lips then looked from the other people on the elevator to me. "I'm..."

"You're what?"

"I'm wet, Walter," she fussed, only she'd forgotten to whisper.

Silence filled the elevator, and the previously chatty patrons craned their necks to see Bree. Some of them laughed while others whispered between themselves. Luckily, it wasn't long before the door opened on our floor.

I grabbed her hand and announced, "Let me go take care of that."

"I know that's right," one of the women said while another man patted me on the back.

The doors closed behind us, and Brielle poked me.

"What?"

"You. Let me go take care of that," she mocked.

"Nobody told your ass to yell that you were wet in front of a bunch of strangers."

She tried to storm off, but I was right behind her. Just as I was about to crowd her body with mine, we both saw Joi Cunningham at my door wearing a highly inappropriate outfit. Bree angled her head up and glared at me. How the hell was I supposed to know Joi would pull something like this. I should have called HR while we were still in McHaven.

"Congratulations you two!" Joi said. She smiled at us both, but it didn't reach her eyes when she regarded Brielle. *Aww shit!*

"Thank you, Joi. I was just heading back to my room." Bree tried to step away, but I held her arm beside me.

"Remember we were supposed to have that conversation." I was thirsty as hell, and I didn't give a damn. I wouldn't blow up Bree's spot if she wasn't ready, but I needed some more of her pussy, the pussy she announced was wet to the people on the elevator less than a minute ago.

Joi's eyes bounced between us. "Is this code talk for some best friend spat?"

"Something like that," I said with my eyes on Brielle.

"It can wait," Bree insisted.

"This won't take long," Joi added.

My jaw was clenched when she slipped out of my grasp. She left me with our sex-starved boss, and now I had a headache.

What were Bree and me? Did I even want a label? The answer to that question was hell no, but for her, I'd do damn near anything. Was she serious about bringing London Bridges around me? I'd known the little homey since he was born, but me and Bree weren't just friends anymore. How the hell would I deal with Lance in the picture, and how would he react to the fact that I was clapping his wife's cheeks?

I smirked and completely forgot Joi was there.

"So you don't mind if I come inside?"

I hadn't heard shit. She mistook my facial expression as an invitation.

Joi was a beautiful woman. She'd aged like fine wine. Joi Cunningham would make some young man very happy, because there was no way someone her age could match her stamina. I could, but I wouldn't. My interest was a few doors down, hopefully waiting for me butt ass naked.

"I do."

Joi's full lips perked up.

"I do mind," I amended. "There's a power dynamic here, and the last thing I want is to be unprofessional with my boss. I love my job."

"I know that, Walt."

"Walter. Please, call me Walter."

"OK."

"While we're in Florida, it's best we communicate via email, phone, or with at least another coworker present."

"That's not necessary," she purred.

She stepped forward, and I moved back. "This is why it's necessary. I'm uncomfortable navigating this conversation. I don't want to upset you, but I'm going inside of my room alone."

Fury flashed across Joi's amber-colored eyes. She wasn't used to rejection, but that was too damn bad.

With an insincere smile on her face, she gritted her teeth and said, "I understand. I'll see you tomorrow."

I quickly entered my room. Was this how women were treated by men who couldn't take a hint? I'd been clear about how uncomfortable I was, and she still wanted to come in.

I grabbed my phone and called Brielle, but the call went straight to voicemail. I'd been fucking her nonstop since we'd left the bar last night. Maybe she had fallen asleep.

Bree

CHANTÉ'S EYES bore into the side of my head. I didn't know why I pretended I hadn't had the best night of my life. I even walked differently.

She'd barged into my suite when I absentmindedly opened the door without checking because I was cooing over a picture of London. I assumed it was Walter who knocked and jumped when I saw her.

She sat on the couch where my best friend and I had enacted delicious, unspeakable acts.

"How was role playing with Chase?" I asked nonchalantly. *Does my room smell like sex?*

"It was as filthy as I hoped it would be," she responded in a dreamy tone. "Bree?"

"Huh?"

"Something is different with you."

"It's the new clothes. Let me change into one of those cute casual outfits you made me buy." I rolled my eyes and scurried out of the room, hopeful she'd drop it.

A lifetime passed in one short weekend. I'd gone from thirsty to thoroughly satisfied at the hands of my very best friend. I was married with no idea how long a divorce would take. There was no way I'd go back to Lance after a sample of what Walter had to offer. Maybe Dizzy and I would remain friends, or maybe we'd continue with more. Either way, I'd been exposed to the world of multiple orgasms. Lance would never have another chance with me.

I was more relaxed now that I'd slipped out of my professional attire. The silk backless, wide-leg jumper kissed my skin with every movement. I breezed back into the main area of the suite to find Chanté's eyes narrowed in my direction.

"Heffa, you weren't going to tell me?" Chanté thundered.

She reached over and pointed to my neck. We were near a mirror, although I had a good idea what she referred to. Walter's passion marks were a deep purple. The bodycon dress I wore hid it for most of the afternoon.

"I…" I wanted to spill, but I didn't know where to start. I also didn't want her to laugh at or judge me.

What if letting Walter fuck me all over my suite was a terrible idea? Chanté wouldn't hold back if she had an opinion. She'd only recently stopped calling out Lance's problematic behavior because her insults were directed at him, but they hurt me in the process.

"Let's go down to the bar. That'll give you time to get your story together. M'kay?"

She snatched her bag and strutted to the door.

"Fine."

I slid my phone and hotel key into my clutch and let my friend drag me out of my suite. I prayed I didn't run into Walter and Joi. If he sent her away, wouldn't he have come to my door to finish what we started?

Chanté filled me in on how she and Chase met at a club. They were my favorite married couple. When we passed Walter's room, my knees quaked. *That man has me wide open. What have I done? And how am I going to explain this to Chanté?*

While we rode the elevator downstairs, she continued about how she'd been on the dance floor dancing with some random guy when Chase arrived. They hadn't worn their wedding rings, so whoever she danced with didn't want to share her with Chase. She insisted the sex they had that night was ten times better because Chase almost came to blows with the other man.

I was over the moon for her. If I ever got married again, I wanted to keep things fresh like they did. The reality was, Walter Simmons wasn't the marrying type. I wouldn't get my hopes up that he would change his perspective, but that man certainly stayed up around me. I snickered.

I owe Melina's ass an apology, because if it's up to me, she won't ever have him again.

"Where are you?" Chanté asked. She held the elevator door open while I stood planted and distracted like a lovesick teen. "Was it that good?"

I nodded. "Girl, yes!" A blush covered my cheeks.

Chanté threw her hands in the air and did a happy dance for me. She jumped up and down then pulled me into a hug. "I knew it! I knew it was fire if you let that man mark you."

We walked arm in arm to the bar, giggling and glowing. I couldn't remember the last time she and I had this much uninterrupted girl chat. We were dressed cute and ready to cut up.

"Brielle?"

Chanté released me and grinned up at Lamar. His smile was what caught my attention last night. It was picture perfect. He also smelled good and kept up a decent conversation.

"And who are you?" Chanté asked.

"I'm a friend of hers. We met last night." He gushed. His eyes raked across my body and Chanté took notice.

"Let me buy you beautiful women a drink?"

"Absolutely," Chanté sang.

Lamar stepped closer to me. When I craned my neck up to see him, he had a ghosted look on his face.

"What happened?" Chanté queried.

"Your babysitter," Lamar snapped.

I stilled. I didn't need to turn around to know Walter Dizzy Simmons had arrived. His scent invaded my nose, and his heat alerted me of his proximity.

"Hey," he said near my ear.

I spun to face him. He was finer than I remembered. *There goes my panties.* Walter made the sensitive area between my legs a sloshy mess.

"Hey, yourself. Where's Joi?" I fussed.

"You look like you found somebody to pass the time." His jaw clenched.

Lamar kissed his teeth as he stormed off.

"What the hell is going on here?" Chanté asked when she overheard our hushed conversation.

"What's going on, Brielle?" he asked me with a smug look on his face.

"Walter and I…" My eyes bounced between my two best friends. Would everything change once the cat was out of the bag? "Ummm."

"Bree used her hall pass," Walter offered.

"I gathered as much from the blurple hickies on her damn neck."

"What is a blurple hickey?" I laughed until Walter stepped beside my angled body and brushed his hard dick against my ass.

"Blue and purple. Don't change the subject. What I can't quite figure out is why the man ran off if the sex was that good."

Walter eyebrows flew up. He was confused, and I was distracted. I never took the time to notice how his mustache and goatee framed his extremely skilled lips. I wanted them on me again.

"Why'd your man run off, Bree Bree?" Walter teased. He practically licked my ear when he spoke.

"It was Walter! Walter Simmons fucked the shit out of me, and I want him to do it again," I blurted.

He leaned down and kissed my neck. I melted. From the depths of my heart, I wanted to have a rational conversation with Chanté, but I'd completely thrown caution to the wind. There was no better feeling than having his mouth or hands on my body.

Chanté's eyes bulged, and her mouth dropped open. She smirked then whipped out her phone.

"What are you doing?" I asked, surprised she hadn't rattled off a billion questions.

"From the way Walter is pressed up against you, I assume y'all are about to kick me to the curb. I'm calling Chase to gossip about this."

She high-fived Walter and pulled me in for a hug. "You deserve to be satisfied. And you deserve for this fine ass work husband, best friend of yours to make your toes curl." She twerked beside me until Chase answered the phone. "We'll talk later, gworl!"

She sashayed away from us with her man on speaker. "You'll never guess who Bree is messing around with?"

"Who, baby?" Chase asked.

"Walt!"

"Nooooooo."

She disappeared and left us alone at the bar.

"What happened with Joi?" To hell with subtlety. Did that cougar ass woman make it inside of his room? I was upset that Lance cheated, because he'd deprived me of sex. Add to that, I stuck around well after I should've left. That was why I slapped him. It never crossed my mind to be envious that Lance shared himself with some other woman, but the idea that another woman might have gotten close to Walter made my blood boil. *I'm tripping. Hard!*

Walter sat on a barstool and pulled me onto his lap. "That's why I need a drink. To answer your real question, she didn't join me inside of my room."

I stuck my nose in the air like I wasn't pressed while he ordered himself a drink.

"You're cute when you're jealous," he teased, pulling my chin in his direction.

"I—"

He leaned his face forward and kissed me, successfully quieting my chatter.

"How long do I have with you until I need to send you back to London Bridges?"

My heart swelled at the mention of my sonshine and at how thoughtful Walter was. He didn't need to be the perfect father figure because London already had a dad, but his being considerate and willing to learn was enough.

"Tomorrow is my last full day. I leave early Tuesday morning. I'm having a ball, but I miss my baby."

"How's he doing away from you?"

"He's preoccupied with Lance and his grandmother."

"Let me see him. I know you got a picture."

"I do!" I squealed. I opened my phone and showed him a picture of London with a ball near his opened mouth and drool dripping over it.

"London Bridges... my man."

I closed my phone and waited as he accepted and nursed his drink.

"About these needs of yours," he started.

I stood abruptly and almost knocked the drink out of his hand.

"What's wrong, baby?" he asked.

I patted his arm although he saw her the moment he looked up.

"Friends, huh?" Zanaé quipped. She was dressed impeccably and was accompanied by her assistant, her bodyguard, and a handsome man I didn't recognize.

"Uh, yes. Well, no. Sort of."

"This I gotta hear," she insisted.

She sat at the corner of the bar near us. Eyes were on her, but no one dared approach with the fierce energy her bodyguard emitted. I reclaimed my seat on Walter's lap, and he gladly welcomed me, kissing the back of my neck when I did.

"Earlier when I asked how long you two had been smashing, you said you were just friends."

"Our boss said that, and technically, we are best friends. We have been for nearly twenty years," Walter offered.

"But you're fucking," Zanaé surmised.

"Nae, stay out of these people business. I'm Rod, Zanaé's friend," he said with a smirk. They were definitely fucking, as she eloquently put it, but given her status, it was probably best they didn't go public with their relationship.

He shook our hands and took a seat beside Zanaé to join the conversation.

"It's complicated," I added.

She twisted her face up. "Sis, is this man fucking you or nah?"

I released a loud belly laugh, and the rest of them joined me. It was insane how drastically my life had changed in twenty-four hours. I'd gone from a broken marriage to having mind-blowing sex with my best friend, to having a casual conversation with a mega star.

"Hell yeah," Walter sang.

"Obviously. She had you so twisted up in our meeting you barely spoke," Zanaé teased. "Babe, he looked like he wanted to fuck her right there."

"Shit, I did," Walter muttered.

"What's the problem?" she pressed.

"Nae thinks she a counselor. You don't have to answer that," Rod announced.

"Technically, I'm married," I admitted.

Everyone's eyes, including the bodyguard, flew to my naked left hand.

"Ohhhh, I see," Zanaé noted.

"It was a loveless marriage," I added.

"A sexless marriage," Walter mumbled.

Her publicist Anton's head popped up.

"He's not lying. Walter was strictly my best friend up until yesterday. He and my other friend convinced me to use this work trip as an opportunity to take a hall pass," I continued.

"For real?" Anton gushed.

I nodded. "But every time someone approached me, Walter's blocking ass was right there."

"Awww," Zanaé sang.

"I legit didn't know why I was so pissed. She'd changed her hair and her clothes and none of these clowns were on her level. When I realized I wanted her, I didn't know how to fess up to it," he admitted.

"Then what?" Zanaé asked with stars in her eyes.

"Y'all know y'all about to be a song, right? Might wanna tell your husband before she makes the video," Rod joked.

"Hush," Zanaé said with her eyes locked on us. "What are you going to do about your husband?"

"I'm getting a divorce. I recently caught him cheating, and before that, he hadn't slept with me in… let's just say a long time."

"Give me my phone," Zanaé said to Anton.

"Already on it. You want to connect her with Nathaniel Brown?" Anton replied with a smirk.

"Who the hell is that?" Walter asked with a little too much bass in his voice.

"Baby," I said and angled my neck to look into his eyes.

He relaxed and threw me a wink. A simple gaze was all it took to reassure him that nobody in Hollyweird could pull me away from him, no matter who introduced us.

"He's a lawyer. One of the best. He doesn't technically practice anymore, but between him and his mentor, he could have your divorce finalized in a matter of weeks," Anton said as he typed on his device.

"Oh my gosh, really?" I asked with tears in my eyes. "There's no way I can afford that type of fancy attorney though." My emotions were all over the place. One of my hesitations to end my marriage was the reality that it would cost an insane amount of money, and the process would take entirely too long.

"It's on me. Y'all are too cute not to be together," Zanaé crooned. She stood, and before I could brace myself, she leaned in and hugged me. "Thank you again for your presentation earlier. It's going to elevate my brand big time, and thank you for sharing your story with me. You didn't have to."

"Of course," I said. I used a napkin to blot my face.

"It's nice to have a conversation without being the one getting asked all the questions for once," she added.

Zanaé took Walter's hand. "Thank you for sharing your lady with me."

"Not a problem. I'm forever indebted to you for helping her take care of her divorce," Walter replied.

Anton asked for my number and email, and in no time, I was CC'd on an email addressed to Nathaniel Brown.

"Let's take one for Instabook," Zanaé volunteered. She whipped out her phone and took an usie with Walter and me. Then Anton and Rod joined while the bodyguard snapped pictures of us laughing and joking about how Lance would be punching the air when he saw this. *Uh oh.*

ten

Walt

BRIELLE LET ME FUCK HER IN EVERY ROOM OF MY SUITE.
We'd been in the shower and the kitchen throughout Sunday night,
but now it was Monday evening, and we were on the balcony with
the ocean as our backdrop. She was facing away from me, and every
time I laid eyes on her toned back and round ass, I had to fight for
my life not to nut. I had one hand between her legs and the other
wrapped firmly around her neck.

"I don't want you to go," I said as she grinded in my lap.

"I don't wanna go either."

"You still gonna let me fuck you in McHaven?" I whined. This
was the first time I begged for pussy. Hell, I didn't need to. Even if I
was between women, it was always by choice and never because I
couldn't get it. Bree was different. I would die if this was the last
time I was inside her.

She moaned, but that wasn't good enough.

"Answer me, Brielle." I emphasized each of my words as I rocked up into her.

She stiffened and met her peak as she cried out, "Yes!"

I wasn't far behind her. "Shit. This pussy is so fuckin' good!" My orgasm took the last shred of strength I had.

She relaxed her damp skin against my chest, letting me slip from inside of her when she did.

"I have an early flight."

"I know."

"What's going to happen with us now, Walt?"

"You're gonna break up with your man," I said, barely able to keep my eyes open. "You think I can order Gatorade with room service? I'm going to need an IV with the way you keep draining me."

She angled her head to see me. "I'm serious. What happens when we're back home and the Melinas of the world start buzzing around?"

"I'm pretty sure you ruined me for anyone else. That's why I acted an ass about them clowns from the airport and downstairs."

She rested her head against my chest. "I never thought I'd see the day when you got jealous." She exhaled. Her satiated state gave me almost as much pleasure as her body. "You still swerved my question. Just because a man doesn't want a woman to be with other men doesn't guarantee he won't see other women."

"Are we seeing each other?" I pressed.

She stilled. I'd already accepted that was what I wanted the night we touched down. Our sexual chemistry only magnified my existing feelings toward her, but since she had a whole ass husband, I didn't want to crowd or overwhelm her.

"After the presentation, I asked if I was more than your hall pass, and you said you would wait and see how the rest of your trip went."

"That was yesterday, Dizzy."

She shivered, so I wrapped my arms around her.

"And it's not like we've done much talking."

"Baby, we've been talking for years without sex as a distraction. I know you, and you know me better than anyone else on the planet. This trip may not have been long, but I've certainly experienced several lifetimes with you in this short amount of time."

She sighed. "That's not what I'm talking about. This dynamic where we sleep together is new. I'm trying to picture how this all plays out."

"Don't overthink it. Hit up Zanaé's contact and get homey to sign the papers."

"Is it that simple?" she asked with an unnecessary amount of sass in her tone.

"Hell yeah."

"We'll see."

I lifted her and stood.

"I can walk, Walter."

"I need you to save your energy. I only got a few hours left to show your pussy who it belongs to."

SHE WOKE up with my hard dick against her ass. Bree had a habit of kicking the covers off when we first fell asleep because she was hot, but at some point during the night, when her body temperature dropped, I would wake up to find her shivering. This time, she woke up on her own. When she did, she felt my erection.

I lifted my arm to check the time on my watch. Bree had to leave for the airport by six a.m. to catch her flight. I couldn't stop my smile when I saw it was only one a.m.

"You back there being nasty?" she murmured.

"Hell yeah. I could be nastier."

She shifted from her side to lie on her back. No matter how many times she put a bonnet on her natural hair, it never stayed in place. Her fuzzy curls were adorable. I'd seen Bree's face consistently for years, but the way it glowed when she smirked at me while she shared my bed made my heart squeeze.

"How?"

"Let me record us."

Her eyes doubled in size, and that sexy mouth of hers fell open, but she didn't say no.

"Trust me; you'll like seeing it played back as much as I will."

I lifted and rummaged through my clothes for my phone. Once I found it, I propped it up on the dresser and hit record.

"As long as you stay on the bed, you'll be in the shot."

She nodded, but hesitation was written across her peanut butter complexion.

I pulled her to the edge of the bed, opened her thighs, then face-planted in my new heaven while she released an exaggerated moan that would taunt me in the recesses of my mind for weeks. The sound radiated from my ears to the bottom of my balls.

Bree's pussy was the best I'd ever tasted, and that was a fact. I slurped and hummed to intensify her pleasure. She writhed on the sheets, and the only reason she couldn't slip away was because of my tight grip on her hips.

"You're gonna love seeing me eat your pussy later."

"I'd rather have the real thing."

She said that now, but in time, she'd be grateful for the ability to revisit our time together.

"Walter. Yes! Please don't stop!"

Her thighs clamped against my head as another tongue-induced orgasm rippled through her body. I lifted and wiped a hand down my goatee. Her eyes were still rolling in the back of her head when I retreated. I slid her body so we were sideways on the bed, to give the camera a full view.

Bree's eyes fluttered open, and they were full of lust. She wanted me again. I'd barely let her breathe since we started this whole hall pass arrangement. If I had to remind her how good we were together, I'd have footage to back me up. Bree and I were a team outside of the bedroom. The fact that she took my dick without complaint was icing on the cake.

I smirked down at her, then flipped her on her stomach. She yelped, and that shit turned me on. I clapped both of her cheeks. Brielle surprised me with how unbothered she was when I tossed her around. She was on all fours with her immaculate ass aimed in my direction.

I pressed on her back, until her arms were stretched out and her face rested against the sheets. I gripped her hips and eased my way inside, unsure of how long I could last if I dove in like I wanted. I sucked in a breath when her wet, tight walls surrounded me.

"Damn, baby," I whined. I'd forgotten the camera was on because I didn't try to disguise how my voice quivered. Her pussy was so good I was on the verge of tears.

When she twerked her cheeks and I saw them bounce against me unrestricted, I stilled. If she moved another muscle, it was a wrap.

"Dizzy?"

Fuck, why she gotta sound so sexy? "Give me a second." It was as though I'd never had sex this intense. Every one of my senses was stimulated. Her moans and whimpers assaulted my ears while her scent infiltrated my nose. The dim light from the next room provided just enough visibility for me to appreciate every thick curve on Brielle's body.

"Walter, I need it, daddy. I need you."

The fuck she say to me?

I rammed into her and increased my pace because either I blacked out or Bree called me daddy.

"What did you call me, Bree Bree?" I accented my words with deep, steady strokes.

"Daddy! I said I need it, daddy."

My balls tingled. She shook her ass again.

"I'm a cum if you keep it up," I admitted.

"I want to feel you cum inside of me."

Bree was nasty, and we'd been reckless about protection. I wanted to pull out to keep us both from something crazy like a hall pass love child, but she reached between her legs and massaged my balls with her soft hands.

"I'm cumming, Bree. Fuck!"

My strokes became erratic, and I roared as I dropped my load into her. *What the fuck am I doing?*

Bree

I MISSED WALTER. We had sex so many times at the *Carnelian* I couldn't tell if we were fucking or making love. It was too soon to consider it making love, but we did love each other. The question was whether the love we had for each other as friends was a good or bad thing when it came to being lovers. *Do I have a husband and a lover?*

I sat in first class with *A Naughty Rendezvous* in my hand, although I'd read the same line for the tenth time. This character having the best sex of her life with someone other than her husband hit too close to home. My book club insisted I finish reading it, but I couldn't. I wanted to judge the main female character when I was no better.

Even if Lance cheated, it didn't justify me sleeping with Walter. I could see that clearly, now that there was space between me and his chiseled abs. Walter's body literally made my mouth water and my center leak. No matter how badly I tried to focus elsewhere, flashes of his mouth on my body and his hands on my ass invaded the forefront of my mind.

An email alert chimed on my opened laptop and dragged me from my sensual torment.

Greetings Brielle Barnes,

A good friend of mine requested my assistance with your divorce. I understand that Thomas is your married name. My colleague did a little research, and you will be as surprised as we were to find that you don't need a divorce attorney. You are in need of a personal injury lawyer which is in my wheelhouse. Lance Darius Thomas is a pseudonym. Lance's real name is Darius Williams.

That means your marriage is invalid. This will likely be a lot to process, but if you are interested in taking legal action, please let me know. What "Lance" has done is considered marriage fraud. You may walk away bypassing the divorce process completely or you have the option to file a suit against him.

I'm available anytime.

Best Regards,

Nathaniel Brown Esq.

Law Professor ENEP

I couldn't breathe. I reread the email several times to make sure I understood what I read. There wasn't enough air on this damn plane, and I needed to get out.

"Ma'am, are you alright?" a concerned stewardess asked.

Sweat dripped from my temples, and my stomach twisted. *What the entire fuck?* I'd known Lance, or whatever his real name was, for a handful of years. Never had he mentioned that he went by a nickname. Was this why he didn't work? Was he fit to be with my son?

Another stewardess joined and handed me a bag. I needed them to give me space. Why were *they* making a big fuss? I was the one whose entire world just flipped upside down.

"I'm a doctor. I can take a look," a woman who was seated across the aisle from me said. We made small talk earlier while we waited to board the plane. "Brielle, right?"

I nodded. My heart rate picked up, and I feared I'd die if I didn't get more air. There were three friendly doctors now and so many stewardesses, then there was black.

Walt

JOI AND AIDEN hadn't made eye contact with me once during the meeting, and the shit was annoying, to say the least. My grown ass had an attitude because my lady was no longer here at my side. I wanted Bree to be mine, and if she hadn't slipped out while I was in a pussy stupor, I would have told her. Maybe it was a good thing I hadn't put that on her before she went home. Chances were, she was already overthinking our situation.

"The presentation with Zanaé went well," Joi said while she wore a smile that didn't reach her eyes.

My colleagues, except for Aiden, whistled and patted me on the back.

"Thanks," I responded.

"He and Brielle have officially sealed the deal," she continued.

Aiden snickered but stopped when he saw the even expression on my face.

My phone rang with a call from an unknown number.

"Is everything OK?" Joi pressed.

I silenced it and nodded.

"Zanaé's team was set to shoot the commercial this week, but it seems she wants both Walter and Brielle to be part of the production. When I told her Brielle returned home, she refused to move forward until she was available."

This time, Joi didn't try to hide the snarl on her deceptively stunning face.

I chuckled to myself. "Bree's going to love that."

Before Joi could object, my phone rang again with the same number. She motioned for me to answer it and continued to address the team while I accepted the call in the back of the conference room.

"Hello."

"Is this Walter Simmons?" a woman whose voice I didn't recognize asked.

"This is he." I wasn't a praying man, but at that moment, I sent up a quick one for my mother. She was in good health, although she wasn't getting any younger. Was this call about my mom?

"Your wife had an accident."

"Wife? You have the wrong number."

"Brielle Thomas. Is she your wife?"

"Yes," tumbled out of my mouth before I could stop myself. Did she say Bree was in an accident?

"Just as we were landing, she lost consciousness. She's at McHaven Medical Center. When can you get here?"

"In an hour if I can get on the next flight."

I disconnected the call and hustled out of the conference room without updating Joi's and Aiden's curious eyes.

I took the stairs two at a time and pummeled through the door connected to the floor of my suite. I ignored the whispers from a couple who rubbernecked in my direction.

What the hell happened to Bree? If she needed someone to count on, she had me. Lance couldn't be trusted, and I'd rather he stay with London until I figured out if she was okay. *Please let her be OK.*

I packed my things in ten minutes. I could book my flight in the rideshare on the way to the airport. My father's name appeared on the screen of my phone. His timing couldn't be worse. There was nothing he and I needed to discuss. I sent his call to voicemail and barged out of the elevator, bumping into someone when I did.

"I'm so sorry," I said as I yanked the small, familiar man up.

"Hall pass?"

I handed him the folder he dropped, then remembered where I'd seen him. "You're the publicist."

"I am. It's Anton," he added. "Your married girlfriend left?"

My stomach twisted. "She did. I'm on my way to see her now."

"Not that it's any of my business, but you look like you just saw a ghost. Is everything OK, hall pass?"

"It's Walt, and Bree had an accident. I need to get to her ASAP." I was halfway down the hall when I called out, "Thank you for asking."

"Ugh! Wait."

I turned around, prepared to tell him he was right that my married girlfriend wasn't any of his business, but he cut in before I could.

"I can have my car get you to the airport and put you on the first flight to your mar—"

"Brielle. Her name is Brielle, but I can't let you do that. You and Zanaé have done enough already." I tried to stay calm, but I was on the verge of a meltdown if I didn't get out of there. I didn't have the bandwidth for pleasantries no matter who his boss was.

"You love her, don't you?"

Despite my urgency to get to Brielle, a smile spread across my face. "Is it that obvious?"

He smirked then rolled his eyes. "Zanaé hasn't stopped talking about the two of you. I'd like to take credit for being a Good Samaritan, but I have no doubt I'll hear an earful if I don't help you." His attention was focused on his phone. I would move heaven and earth to get to Bree, so I stood, ready to accept yet another handout.

"Type your first and last name, date of birth, and social security information here," he said, shoving his smartphone into my hands.

I did as he asked, and before I could process what happened, I was shuffled out of the hotel and into an all-black luxury vehicle. The driver didn't attempt small talk, which was a relief. My knee bounced double-time, and the worst-case scenarios crowded my mind's eyes.

By the time we arrived at the airport, I'd convinced myself Bree had gotten a life-threatening diagnosis. I hustled into the airport with my carry-on, still wearing my business casual attire. My feet cursed me out with every step. If I had time, I'd change in the bathroom.

"I need your license," the desk attendant said when I checked in.

She typed my information into the computer and gasped at what she saw on the screen.

"Is there a problem with my flight?" It had been booked less than thirty minutes ago. Zanaé was rich and famous, but even her reach had limits.

"Your flight will leave in twenty minutes. One of our attendants will escort you to the private lounge."

I couldn't concentrate on a single thought to save my life.

"Private lounge?"

"Yes. Our private charters have an entirely different boarding protocol. There's no need for you to search for a gate or bother with TSA. Enjoy your flight, Mr. Simmons."

I ran a hand through my locs. Under any other circumstance, I would have been on cloud nine. *Right now, I need to get to Bree.* It didn't matter whether my mode of transportation was luxury or if I had to ride a donkey.

Bree

MY STOMACH CHURNED at the unfamiliar smell. I wasn't a fan of flying, but first class had never been this bad. My eyes flew open when a beep on a nearby machine rang in my ears. *Am I in a hospital?* This was my punishment for that damn hall pass.

Was Walter here with me? I focused my eyes on the man seated next to my bed. This was a hospital all right, but that wasn't Dizzy.

"Lance?"

"I was worried sick about you, baby."

Baby?

He leaned down, and when he was inches from my face said, "I love you. I love you and I'm so sorry. I don't know what London and I would do without you."

Lance kissed me deeply. For a moment, I relaxed into his kiss because I was caught up in finally being seen by him. It had been months since he acknowledged my presence, and now the man I married wanted me. Realization of why I was in the hospital pressed into my chest like a weighted vest. Zanaé's fancy attorney revealed that the man who fathered a child with me was not who he said he was. His name wasn't even Lance.

I pushed his arm away with the little strength I had. Lance barely budged. He stroked the side of my face with one hand and squeezed my ass with the other.

"I want us to try again. I miss you."

Is he for real? "I'm done," I growled.

His beautiful face twisted in confusion. "What you mean? You trying to divorce me?" His voice screeched when he asked.

I glared at him. Thank God for Walter. He'd exposed me to how I deserved to be handled. Had I not taken Walt up on his offer to be my hall pass, I could have easily fallen for Lance's lame attempt to woo me. The moment I displayed an ounce of resistance, his true nature showed through.

A snarl spread across his lips—the lips I'd dreamt about, wishing he'd use them on me like he did in the past.

"I've gotten accustomed to a certain lifestyle."

Now I wore a smirk on my face. Lance wasn't interested in trying again; he was a man digger trying to secure the bag. Walter was right once again. Lance, or Darius rather, was my wife, just as Walt described in his blog. He hadn't moved his body off my bed, and his face was still close.

"There's no need for a divorce," I said sweetly.

Shards of glass against the sterile floor startled us both. Walter stood in the door beside a shattered vase of a dozen large, stemmed roses. *How did he get here? Wasn't he still working in Florida?* His jaw was clenched as he regarded Lance's proximity to my face.

Did he see Lance kiss me? Did he hear me say I didn't need a divorce? I didn't need one because legally we weren't married.

"Walter…"

He dropped his shoulders and backed out of the door.

"Excuse me, nurse. I need someone to clean up the broken glass in room four seventeen," he said in a strained voice.

He was gone. My inability to breathe returned. I had little patience to deal with Lance. I couldn't cope with Walter thinking I wanted my ex, and more than anything, I wanted my baby boy.

eleven

Walt

I TORE MY LIVING ROOM UPSIDE DOWN. A PUZZLE I'D SPENT over a month working on was strewn across my floor beneath what used to be my coffee table. I hadn't had an outburst like this since I was a teenager. Growing up, I was miserable when my dad was home and angry when he was gone. While he could no longer lay hands on my mother, he also wasn't around when I needed him.

This was why I had no faith in marriage. Bree would remain with a man who was beneath her when she could have the princess treatment she deserved with me. My own mother allowed herself to stay with my father because they were married. It made absolutely no sense. I meant it when I blogged that black women didn't need a wife. What they needed was support.

In my fit of rage, I hadn't bothered to lock up. When I threw myself onto the couch to catch my breath, I locked eyes with Mason Frazier, who stood and watched the scene unfold before him.

"The hell are you doing here?" I asked, winded.

He rubbed a hand down his full salt and pepper colored beard.

"I came to check on you."

"What? Why?" I hated feeling like an adolescent, but I was a whiny mess whenever I was in this man's presence.

"I wanted to check on you. You probably meant to ignore my call again, but I overheard you admit to loving your best friend. Are you sneaking around with Brielle?"

I was, but not anymore. Brielle went on and on about how she wanted God to bless her marriage. Maybe her time with me gave her the reset she needed and the glow necessary to regain his attention. A lump formed in my throat.

"Why does it matter?" Exhaustion coursed through my body. The responsibility to clean my place was mine, but the release it provided was worth it.

"Contrary to what you might be telling yourself, I care about you, Walter. You and Brielle have known each other since college. I would hate for that to change because you decided to have an affair with her. By the looks of it, I'm too late."

"She said she was going to leave him," I muttered.

"You're smarter than this, Walter." Glass crunched under his feet as he moved toward the couch. He slowly took a seat at the opposite edge where I sat staring in disbelief.

"Nobody leaves their marriage for an affair, not even women."

"It's not like that," I tried.

"Well, why the hell are you breaking all your shit?"

I sighed. "I don't have to explain this to you."

"That's true, but what other option do you have?"

"You wanna be a dad *now*?" I countered.

He sat and turned his body to face me. I inherited my imposing demeanor from him. If people were fearful around me, they would shit themselves being under Mason's death glare. His jaw clenched, and I didn't miss him steady his breath.

"I've always wanted to be your dad. I ain't never left."

"But you did. When you finally stopped terrorizing my mother, you left me too."

"What?" His death glare was replaced with large, bewildered eyes that mirrored mine.

"I saw you... I saw you wrap your hands around my mother's neck and strangle her until she lost consciousness. I saw you push her around and slap her when she stepped out of line."

The blood drained from his face. He stood and created space between us.

"Your grandfather told you that?"

"Nope. If Pop Pop knew you hit my mom, he would've shot you."

He leaned against the wall and scrubbed his finger back and forth between his lip and his nose. His mannerisms reminded me of myself, despite how little time I spent with him.

"And I would've deserved it. This ain't an excuse, but I'm an— I'm an alcoholic."

"What?" *How has this never come up? I don't remember seeing him drink.*

"I hid alcohol in water bottles and soda cans because I never wanted you to see me like that. I thought I was careful, even with the awful way I treated your mom. It makes sense now why you hated me so much. Looks like the apple doesn't fall far from the tree."

I shot to my feet. "I ain't nothing like you."

He looked around my place and then back at me.

"I'm not a drunk, and I don't hit women!"

"I'm talking about anger. It's anger that will drive you to act in ways you'll regret in the future."

I blinked back frustrated tears. I was the truth teller. This was about him, not me, and he was the last person I would speak to about my rage.

"When did you get clean?"

"I joined one of those twelve step programs after Grace put me out."

Brielle's ringtone sounded from underneath my jacket. My lip automatically lifted and connected with my nose. I missed Bree, and I left before I found out if she was physically okay.

"You still love her?" I asked, silencing Bree's call.

"More than anything in this world next to you."

He maintained eye contact, and I didn't miss his glassy eyes as he spoke of his love for us. He sure as hell had a funny way of expressing it.

Mason cleared his throat. "Will you pick up when I call you next time?"

I nodded. My father turned toward the door and, with his back to me, added, "Your mother was involved when I met her."

"She was?"

"Yep." He craned his neck in my direction with a smirk on his face. Apparently, I'd gotten my charm from him too.

"What did you do?"

"Convinced her I was the best choice, then I married her. I'll talk to you soon, Walter."

Bree

THE KID DOCTOR who was assigned to me at the hospital assured me that I had been overly stressed and exhausted. Fainting from a panic attack wasn't common, but it was the only reasonable explanation he and his team had.

"I'll make sure she gets her rest," Lance said, ignoring my request for him to allow my mom to pick me up and take me home.

Once I was dressed and discharged, we spent most of the drive in silence.

"What did you mean when you said we didn't need a divorce?" Lance asked, breaking into my deep contemplation.

"What did you mean about being accustomed to a certain lifestyle?" I shot back. *He wants to be kept like the man digger he is. Little does he know, he won't get a dime of my money.*

Everyone was used to mousy Bree, who relented for the sake of peace. I didn't make a habit of employing sarcasm to get my point across, but my son's father pushed me too far this time. He didn't have an answer.

"Will you be honest with me?" I asked. I only agreed to let him drive me because I wanted to see London, and my baby was with Lance's mother.

"Yes. I don't want any more lies between us."

I pursed my lips and prayed for the strength not to put my hands on him again.

"What's your name?"

"Lance." He turned his head in my direction briefly with an unassuming smile on his face.

I continued to watch the McHaven wooded scenery through the passenger window. It was an ever-present reminder that I was no longer in Florida. I missed Walter almost as much as I missed my sonshine.

"Tell me the name printed on your birth certificate." My voice was void of emotion now. I was done with him the moment my trip started. Nathaniel Brown's email was simply confirmation that I could no longer overlook the fact my marriage was over—a marriage that wasn't recognized by the law.

He parked in the driveway of his mother's home. *Has that wench Emma been here? How's Lance going to react about Walter and me? Why the hell hadn't he told me about his real name?*

"Who told you that?"

Wrong answer, asshole!

I reached for the door but stopped when Lance gently grabbed my arm. We were silent for several moments.

"I have a record. It kept me from getting any real work in the past, so I changed it."

"Don't flip this like you're certain it would have been a deal breaker for me. We went over a year without having sex, and I stayed. I would have done everything in my power to help you find a job or a program for felons. Why not tell me? You married me with a fake name."

"Why does it matter now, Bree?"

"I slept with Walter," I blurted. I wasn't sure why I told him at that moment.

I saw the color drain from Lance's handsome face. He gripped the steering wheel and dropped his shoulders.

"You a hypocrite."

"Excuse me?" *Is he for real?*

"You put me out over Emma, knowing you was fucking your *friend* this whole time."

I shifted my body to face him. "I begged you to touch me. Do you know what that was like for me?"

He tried to respond, but I continued.

"I slept with Walter for the first time this weekend—not that it's any of your business. Before that, we were just friends."

Lance scratched his neck. "You did this to make me jealous? To get my attention?"

I rolled my eyes.

"It worked," he said and licked his lips.

"You're all over the place. First you refuse to have sex with me, then I find out you're in a relationship with someone who referred to me as your ex-wife. I end up in a hospital bed stressed because I don't know who the hell I married, and you decide that's the appropriate time to tell me you're accustomed to a certain lifestyle like you're going to sue me for alimony. Now I'm admitting I slept with my best friend, and you expect me to believe you can look past it?"

"I'm trying—"

"No, you're not. I'm done, and I'm only interested in coparenting with you from here on out."

I got out of his car and slammed the door when I did. There was nothing else I needed to say to him. London had gone too many days without me, and that was my highest priority.

Walt

MY DAD DROPPED a bomb on me when he popped up at my house last week. My mom had been involved with someone else. Mason and I talked again over the phone since he found me tearing my shit up. He apologized for everything I saw when I was a kid. He called it an amends. I forgave him in my head, but it would take much longer for my heart to catch up to this version of Mason Frazier.

I hadn't seen Brielle since I flew home to McHaven after receiving the call that she'd had an accident. Was she okay? What had London been up to? I missed his drooling, chunky face. I'd been tormented with how sweetly Bree spoke to Lance. She told him they didn't need a divorce. My head throbbed at the memory of his hands on her ass.

She called twice in the last week, but I sent them both to voicemail. I couldn't bear her breaking up with me to go back to her neglectful husband. In an uncharacteristic move, she took that week off, leaving me alone at M3.

Joi wasn't pleased with my abrupt departure from Florida but hadn't acknowledged it thus far.

I sat in my office with my eyes trained on my computer. I wasn't working, but I didn't want anyone to try to make small talk with me. I only came into the office to get some fresh air since I'd been holed up in my place far too long.

I still wanted Brielle, even though she didn't want my ass. Maybe I wasn't as charming as I thought I was. I hadn't imagined our time together. Her body obeyed my every command, and she'd been eager to participate. Maybe I'd miscalculated what I meant to her.

I redirected my attention to my phone. I had a video of our last night together. My finger itched to watch it, but it would only exacerbate my longing for her. *Fuck!*

A light knock sounded at my door. Bree wore tight, chocolate leather pants that covered most of her shoes. The oversized brown button up covering her immaculate ass made the look professional. This was another outfit from her makeover. *Damn!*

When she stepped inside, her eyes held a sadness that wasn't there when I was with her. Brielle's body made my pants tighten and my tongue twitch. I gritted my teeth. Had she given Lance what I stamped my name on?

"Hey," she started.

I stood and was in her space in a split second. She stared up at me wordlessly. I gritted my teeth again but found myself pulling her into my arms, despite my urge to confront and interrogate her. My entire being wanted to make my intentions clear.

Instead, I allowed my eyes to survey her body for bandages or bruises.

"Are you OK, Brielle?" I asked.

"I fainted on the plane. I'm fine."

My eyes widened, and I loosened my grip on her body to find her eyes.

"Walter, I'm good. I want to talk about what you walked in on," she said as she slipped from my embrace to close my office door.

When she did, I got an unobstructed view of her ass. The blouse was powerless to fully hide her curvy silhouette. She turned in time to catch me admiring her impressive backside.

I wore a sheepish grin and tugged at my tie.

"I don't need to know the details of your relationship with him. You're my best friend. All I want is for you to be taken care of."

My stomach jerked. Had her time with me saved her marriage? Was a weekend hall pass enough motivation for her husband to step up? Did Lance notice her new glow and carefree nature?

"Liar," she accused. She poked me in the center of my chest.

I tipped her chin up and placed an unhurried kiss to her juicy lips. She didn't protest or push me away. Bree returned my kiss with an equal amount of passion. I only pulled back because the glass doors of my office ruined any chance for privacy between us.

"It's not fair for me to be your side piece."

She giggled, but I was as serious as a heart attack, although my choice of words didn't stress that fact. I loved the sound of Bree's laughter. I wanted nothing more than to see her happy, but my heart was involved, whether I wanted it to be or not. This was no longer a hall pass for me. If I kept up this affair while she went back and forth to her husband, I'd end up with a broken heart.

"I said we don't need a divorce, because technically, we aren't married."

Before I could fire off a million questions, Bree continued.

"You remember Zanaé's assistant emailed their lawyer?"

I nodded. Anton was more efficient than she knew.

"I saw the lawyer's response to the email on my flight back to McHaven. He said he did a little digging, and Lance's real name is Darius."

"The fuck?"

"Yeah, I know. Because he lied on the marriage certificate, the marriage is null. What you walked in on was him threatening to sue for spousal support if I left him. I lovingly informed him that there would be no divorce, and therefore, there would be no exchange of money."

My fists balled at my sides as I tried to process this new information. He had a lot of nerve to try to intimidate my damn woman. At least I wanted Bree to be mine, especially now that I found out she wasn't married.

I kissed her again. "Do you have any idea how bad I've wanted to watch the flick we made?"

She crossed her arms across her chest, and like a perv, my eyes focused on her titties. When I finally lifted my gaze, her lips formed a mischievous grin.

"What?"

"I don't believe you," she purred.

"I couldn't do it. I swear."

She opened her mouth to respond but was interrupted by another knock at my door. I struggled to keep my hands off her. Brielle wasn't married. Her name was still Brielle Kari Barnes, just as it should be.

Aiden glared at us. I barely paid him any attention, and for the first time, neither did Bree.

"Everyone is gathering in the break room to see Sean off," he said flatly.

"OK," I returned. It was painful to tear my eyes from the masterpiece that was Bree to engage with Aiden's hating ass, but I was at work.

Once Aiden was gone, I said, "We're not finished with this conversation, Barnes."

Her eyes closed briefly as if she wanted me as bad as I longed for her.

"Be good, Walter." She rubbed her hand down the center of my chest before leaving my office, and I was positive I would explode in anticipation. I couldn't wait to get back inside of my best friend.

Bree

Our coworker Sean loved his gift and the spread I made for his going away party. He was a fellow employee who wasn't appreciated for his diligence with the company. Sean kept to himself, for the most part, but in terms of collaboration, he'd always been top tier.

I was on cloud fifteen—cloud nine simply wasn't high enough—as I re-entered my office. I'd made the situation clear to Walter, and he still wanted me. I had a blush on my face as images of our sinful acts—the ones that were captured on video—replayed in my mind. Contradictorily, I had my praise and worship music on in the background.

I hadn't tidied up my space since before the new year. I'd been so stressed about caring for London and plotting on ways to save my marriage that the clutter in my office had been low on my to-do list. Today was the right time to finally do something about it. Not only had I taken time off, but I'd been fortunate enough to spend quality time with London. Our trips to the library and children's museum had made me love him more than I thought was possible.

I hummed while I tossed paper into the recycling bin. This song was about taking shackles off my feet so I could dance. I bounced and let the music minister to my soul.

"Now you want to praise God. After the immoral things you've done?"

"Mama?" My hand flew to my chest as I turned down the music to orient myself. My mother had been to M3 maybe twice in all the years I'd worked here. Did she know I slept with Walter?

I faced her like an unruly toddler. Her presence alone was terrorizing enough to send me back to a childlike state.

"You shot at Lance?"

Her words snapped me from our normal dysfunctional cycle. I kissed my teeth. "I didn't shoot at him. Is that what he told you?"

I plopped in my chair and motioned for her to do the same.

"I'll stand."

"Suit yourself. Lance had his pants down and was sexually entertaining another woman when I fired a warning shot for him to get out of my house."

My mother's eyes bulged, and she quickly took a seat.

"His name isn't even Lance, Mama."

My mother's eyes were all over the place. "It doesn't matter," she said, regaining her faux 'rise above' countenance.

"Yes, it does." I recounted everything I'd learned concerning Lance and his fake identity. I also relayed to her how my marriage wasn't legal as a result.

"Your dad could remarry you," she insisted.

"Do you hear yourself, Mom? I'm not a saint, and I'm not Jesus. Why is it so important to you that I stay with a man who doesn't want me?"

"Of course, Lance wants—"

"He hasn't touched me in over a year, he had an affair, and he threatened to sue me for alimony when I told him it was over. I deserve better."

She narrowed her eyes. "You women today are so entitled. My mother was married for forty years."

I blew out a breath. "I don't want to be disrespectful, Mama, but I'm tired of biting my tongue for people who don't respect me. Grandma *couldn't* divorce Grandpa. Times were different then. Men served as protection, and they were the primary breadwinners. If she made all the money, I doubt she would have stuck around."

My mother shot to her feet. "You watch your damn mouth." She clapped her hand over her lips. In all my years of living, my mom never swore. She was a good Christian woman. With one last disapproving scowl, she left my office.

I sat there in a daze. I yearned for the type of relationship

Walter and Chanté had with their mothers. Mine was likely venting her frustrations to my father who wouldn't call me. Instead, he'd hold in his gripes and unload them on me the moment I set foot on his property.

Dizzy's mom was more supportive of me than my own. *Does she know I slept with her son?* I grinned to myself. As if my thoughts conjured him up, my phone buzzed.

WALT DIZZY:

I need it

ME:

You need what?

I had an idea of what he desired, but I wanted him to say it. In lieu of a response, he sent a picture. His untamed locs were all I could see of him while his head rested between my legs. It was a screengrab of our homemade movie. My mouth fell open.

ME:

My place or yours

WALT DIZZY:

You serious?

ME:

Yes

Before I could pack my belongings, he was at my door. His wide frame leaned against the area my mother had just vacated.

"Can you drive to my place?"

I nodded.

He glanced down at his watch.

"You have somewhere else you need to be?" I teased.

"No. I just want to make sure I don't keep you from London Bridges."

My already soggy panties were now ruined. Walter had the good sense to be concerned with my son. I couldn't wait for him to reenact the image he sent to my phone.

"Just the two people I need to see," Joi said from behind Walter.

She wasn't curt in her remark, but she certainly hadn't been warm and fuzzy with us. There was no doubt in my mind that Aiden had filled her in on what he saw that day in Florida. Joi wanted Walter for herself, and she'd always seen our friendship as a threat. Now that our platonic relationship had developed into a wild affair, would she make life hell for me?

She and Walter stepped inside of my office with her closing the door as she did.

"Zanaé's team swears she wants you two on set when she films the commercial." Joi rolled her eyes.

I wore a smirk as my eyes bounced between hers and Walter's. His jaw clenched, and I couldn't tell if he was simply bothered by Joi's presence or if he was pissed because our plans had been delayed.

"We need to get this commercial shot before *CocoaKiss Cosmetics* launches their highly anticipated new lip gloss." Joi shifted her focus to me. "How quickly can you arrange childcare?"

I picked up my phone as if the answers to Joi's questions were there. Another getaway would be fabulous, especially since Walt would be by my side. The issue was now that I didn't need a divorce from Lance and my mother was displeased with my behavior, I didn't want either of them handling London.

Walter motioned for me to come and speak to him near the door. He didn't give a damn what Joi thought about it. She had the good sense to scroll through her phone while we had a side conversation.

"Bring Baby Bridges with us," he urged.

I titled my head to look up at him. "Huh?"

"I miss him."

My mouth fell open as it often did. With a mischievous smile on his face, he used his pointer finger to close it. "I know they just took time off for vacation, but see if Chanté and Chance want to bring Hakeem. I'll pay for everything."

I released a tortured breath when I spun around to face Joi. "I can have an answer for you in less than an hour."

Joi lifted with a disapproving scowl on her face at the sight of our matching blush. There was one thing she valued above her interest in my Walter and that was making money.

"Call me right away. The sooner I can get the two of you to her, the sooner we all get paid." With one last evil eye aimed in my direction, she left us alone in my office.

twelve

Walt

WITH ALL THE PREPARATION FOR ANOTHER WORK TRIP, I hadn't had the pleasure of being back between Bree's legs since our return to McHaven. She was busy rallying Chanté and Chase, who were both willing to tag along to watch London while Bree and I worked. I had to beg them to let me pay, and once I reminded them I was a single man who wanted to impress my new lady, they relented.

Bree and I hadn't spoken about a label for what we were, but whenever I discussed her, I referred to her as my lady. It was a relief that legally she wasn't married, although I was smart enough to know Lance's ass would always be in the picture to raise their son. We rarely spoke about him. Now that he couldn't get her money, he didn't pose a threat to her emotional state, which was all I cared about.

Everyone was assured that Zanaé's driver would pick each of us up from our respective homes and transport us to the airport where we would be flown to one of Zanaé's properties. This estate featured the studio where the commercial would be filmed. I was packed and decided the best way to pass the time was to text Brielle some nasty shit.

ME:

What you got on?

BRIELLE KARI BARNES:

I almost dropped a carton of milk. I'm getting London fed and rushing around. This is not sexy.

ME:

I bet it is. Let me see you.

BRIELLE KARI BARNES:

I'm serious, Dizzy. I need to focus, so I can be on time

ME:

It's a private jet, they'll wait.

BRIELLE KARI BARNES:

eye roll emoji

ME:

Video message

I SENT a snippet of our video together. It was the part where I clapped both her cheeks then hit it from behind. I'd zoomed enough that her twerk session could be seen. I would've paid money to see her face when she saw it.

BRIELLE KARI BARNES:

I tripped over one of London's toys just so you know. He thought it was hilarious

ME:

I'm sorry

BRIELLE KARI BARNES:

No, you're not. I know you're over there
laughing too.

ME:

Let's make another video

She didn't respond to my last text. I was picked up by the driver first, then we stopped to get Chanté, Chase, and Hakeem. Brielle and London were the closest to the airport and therefore the last stop.

"What up, young king?" I said as I greeted Hakeem.

He smiled brightly as he took a seat beside me.

"Hey, Walter. Thank you again." Chanté gushed.

I waved her off as I dapped up Chase.

"Seriously, thank you," Chase insisted.

"All this time I thought you were calling me young Keem," Hakeem admitted. The four of us fell into boisterous laughter as we pulled up to Brielle's address. The driver attempted to exit the car, but I quickly halted his efforts.

"I got it," I said halfway out of the door.

Just before I stepped out, Chanté added, "I know that's right."

I knocked lightly on Bree's front door with my heart beating double time. When she opened it, holding London in her arms, my heart slowed. They were all it took to calm me down.

"Will you be my lady, Bree Bree?"

Her eyes were wide as she stared at me with her mouth wide open.

"Bree," London cooed.

She scrunched her mouth up playfully and turned to London. "Mommy."

I reached for him, and he kicked his chunky legs until he was successfully in my arms. I placed a quick kiss on his wet cheek.

"What's up, London Bridges?"

His response was unintelligible, but I was positive he was happy to see me too. I accepted her bag and the car seat, so her hands were free to wheel her carry-on and London's colorful luggage.

"You gonna make us miss our flight," I teased, because I wouldn't budge until she agreed to be with me.

Bree rolled her eyes. "Can we talk about this on the plane?"

I shook my head.

Bree's slanted eyes bounced from her baby boy to me.

"London Bridges, can I be your mommy's man?"

"Walter…"

She stopped when London nodded his head vigorously. He wore a big, mostly toothless smile as drool dripped down his chin. I used his handkerchief styled bib to take care of that for him.

"Looks like you're outnumbered."

"How are you gonna use my baby against me?"

I stepped into her space and placed a kiss on her round lips. "Please, baby?"

When I pulled back, her eyes were closed, and her lips were parted. "Yes," she said on an exhale. "Of course, I will."

My cheeks hurt from smiling so hard. Both Brielle and her son held different corners of my heart. She'd just made me the happiest man in the world.

Bree

CHANTÉ and I couldn't chat the way we wanted with our guys and the children in tow, so we took to text messages as the next best thing.

CHANTÉ:

You know Walter's in love right

ME:

That's just afterglow

CHANTÉ:

Afterglow is for after sex. You said you
haven't been with him since you got back.
Does he know about Lance?

I peered up from my phone and nodded at her. The wide grin she threw in my direction elicited a schoolgirl giggle from me.

ME:

He asked me to be his lady

"Awww," Chanté said instead of texting.

I found Walter's eyes on me. The smirk he wore was sexy. Did he know that Chanté and I were talking about him?

I went back to my phone to scold my other best friend when I saw a message from Walter.

WALTER:

I want to make another video with my lady

The butterflies in my stomach fluttered as I subconsciously pulled my bottom lip between my teeth.

ME:

I haven't watched the first video. I'll probably be too embarrassed to see myself being that uninhibited with you

My head flew up at the sound of Chanté's gasp.

"You OK, Mama?" Hakeem asked. He'd grown into such a respectful and attentive young man.

Chuckles from both Chase and Walter confirmed my worst fear. I took another glance down at my phone and saw that I'd texted the group chat with Walt, Chanté, and Chase about our sex tape. Heat covered my cheeks at the realization that everyone saw my message.

WALTER:

It's okay, baby. We're all grown

CHANTÉ:

I know that's right

CHASE:

I'm happy for y'all

"All right," I blurted, unable to take their supportive messages any longer. My embarrassment subsided with one look at London, who was already knocked out. I hoped he wouldn't have issues flying and that he would have a great trip, despite my intentions of being nasty with my new boyfriend.

THE PRIVATE JET was more enjoyable than anything I'd ever had the pleasure of experiencing. It was more like a brief get-together in someone's luxurious living room than a flight. The only reminder that we were in the air were the brief check-ins from the stewardess. London slept through the entire ride.

The six of us would stay at a nearby resort for the duration of our trip. London and I had our own room, with Walter next door, and Chanté, Chase, and Hakeem across the hall. I kept an eye on a curious London as I simultaneously unpacked for the two of us. I fed and changed my baby, then turned him over to Chanté since our business was to take place at the front end of our trip which was truly a relief.

I doubted I would be of much use to anyone once Walter got his hands on me, from the sinful looks he continued to throw my way throughout our travel. The handoff with London was easy since Hakeem was ready and willing to entertain my baby.

"I'll be back, handsome boy," I cooed.

"Bye, Mama," he said as clear as day.

"We're fine. Go and try to focus on your work," Chanté said with a mischievous grin on her face. "I can't believe you made a sex tape," she whispered in my direction. I shrugged innocently. The cat was out of the bag, and there was no denying it now.

I kissed the top of London's head and shuffled back to my room to change. I selected an outfit that was presentable enough to be in the presence of a superstar but also sensual enough to keep Walter's attention, not that it would take much. He was invested, and he wasn't shy to show it.

He and I met in the lobby and were once again transported in style from the resort to the location of the shoot. Walter pulled me into an embrace and wouldn't stop telling me how beautiful I was and how good I smelled.

"Thank you," I returned with a blush.

The way he stood and regarded me should've been against the law. His fitted blue button up and white slacks draped his toned shape perfectly. I was grateful Zanaé already had a man with how fine Walter looked today with his long locs hanging down his shoulders.

We rode in a comfortable silence. At one point, he grasped my hand and intertwined his fingers with mine. He brought my hand to his mouth and kissed my knuckles, sending sensations of pleasure throughout my body. My new man threw a wink at me, and my lips parted automatically.

"You good, Bree Bree?" he asked in a voice that made me weak in the knees.

I nodded, fearful of what might fall out of my mouth if I spoke.

We arrived at Zanaé's estate, and if I were to describe the home as breathtaking, it would truly have been an understatement. The seven-thousand square foot, Mediterranean-style mansion was opulent and fit for a princess.

Unsurprisingly, we were promptly greeted by someone from Zanaé's staff. He was an older gentleman who was dressed to the nines. His eyes brightened as he allowed them to skirt over my figure appreciatively. Walter pulled me into his side, causing me to giggle at his jealousy toward a man who likely had a decade on my father.

"You must be Walter and Brielle."

There was unnecessary tenderness in the way he enunciated my name. He extended his hand in Walter's direction, and when Walter didn't make a move to take it, I stole a glance at my best friend turned lover turned man who instead offered the older man a halfhearted nod.

I accepted his hand in place of Walter's and responded with, "That's correct. What is your name?"

"Arthur Abbott."

When Arthur attempted to lift my hand to his lips, Walter cleared his throat. The gesture caused Arthur to release me.

"It's right this way."

When he turned toward the estate entrance, I elbowed Walter

who shrugged. He leaned in and whispered, "I'll fuck an old man up over you."

I giggled at his territorial nature. "I must have really put it on you," I returned.

Walter and I were given a brief tour. It was difficult to pay attention with the brazen looks my man gave me any time I peered in his direction. Then there were the not so accidental ways he brushed up against me any chance he could. We were led to an area disconnected from the main living space, although it was still attached to the property. I gasped at the sight of the immaculate studio space.

It was like something out of a movie. My eyes were wide with wonder as I peered at the complicated equipment with a gazillion buttons. There was a microphone and chair on the other side of a large soundproof glass. Speakers were built into the walls providing a flawless sound that tickled my ears.

Zanaé's team was busy at work setting up around her while she sang a song that stopped me in my tracks. She bellowed melodic runs that were angelic. The words started as hums then progressed from a soprano range that deepened to more of a baritone rasp.

"He was my justified," she began in a sweet, calm tone, *"Hall Pass."*

My hand flew to the center of my chest. Zanaé sang a song about our situation. I gazed up at Walter whose eyes were already trained on me. For this man to have a crush on the popstar, he'd barely paid her any mind in the times we'd shared space with her. Walter leaned down and placed a quick peck to my lips. Our eyes flew to her when Zanaé squealed.

"My favorite couple." She crooned into the microphone from her position on the other side of the glass.

With her professional linebacker-built bodyguard acting as her shadow, she hopped up from the stool and eagerly sashayed toward us. Goliath was stealthy as he was somehow able to give her space while making his presence known. Walter may have been unbothered, but I still hadn't adjusted to the star power Zanaé possessed. Not only was the woman beautiful, but she was incredibly sweet and selfless with her resources.

Zanaé pulled us both into a thruple hug, causing Walter to release a deep, throaty chuckle.

"Thank you for having us," he offered as he slipped from her embrace while maintaining his hold on me.

She gave us a knowing once over when she said, "I told Rod this wasn't a one-weekend thing with the two of you. Nathaniel got you straightened out that fast, sis?" She directed her question to me, and I didn't miss Walter tighten when she did.

"How much time do you have?" I asked with my bottom lip tucked between my teeth.

Despite our company, Walter leaned down and said, "Please release your bottom lip. It's making me jealous."

A blush covered my cheeks.

Zanaé smirked and announced, "Give us a minute."

With that one directive, the entire space cleared in a matter of seconds. She led us to what had to be a custom-made sofa that extended the length of two walls.

"Spill." She gushed.

"First, thank you again for having us. When Joi said you insisted we be on set, I was shocked and over the moon," I started.

"Bree, I like you and all, but if you don't get to the point, I can't be held responsible for my actions," Zanaé said flatly.

Walter, who hadn't been keyed into our conversation because of his constant drooling and staring at my ass, let out another hearty laugh. He lifted his hands when I glared at him.

"Let the woman know what she wants," he teased.

I recounted the events surrounding the information I received from Nathaniel Brown about Lance. Zanaé's eyebrows were furrowed as she listened.

"But more importantly, Walter and I are officially a couple."

She placed her hands on her cheeks with sheer adoration. "That makes this song even more special. Of course, Rod tried talking me out of creating a love song inspired by what he referred to as a sneaky link, but my gut told me there would be more to your story."

There were happy tears in her eyes when she spoke.

"I love love. I'm a hopeless romantic," she said as she swiped a tear from her eye. "And you," she said as she hit Walter on the arm.

"What I do?" he teased.

"It was obvious from the way you looked at her during the presentation that you were gone over her. I'm just glad you didn't let her go back to that trifling ex of hers." Zanaé rolled her eyes at the mention of Lance.

"That wasn't gonna happen on my watch," Walter asserted.

She stood and bounced excitedly. "Let's get started, shall we?"

Walter

I DIDN'T DOUBT that Zanaé's ad would do numbers, but seeing it being created in person was like watching history being made. The fans would eat up the song she wrote for me and Brielle. I had to admit it was a bop, and while I no longer had a crush on Zanaé, this was a song I would certainly wear out once I got my hands on it.

Just as Bree suggested back in McHaven, Zanaé had the lip gloss propped up on the music stand. She was in a soundproof booth with one headphone on her ear while the other was pushed back. She purred the same justified hall pass line when Ashy Peeping Arthur brought us back here. I didn't give a damn how old he was; he would keep his eyes off my woman or catch these hands. *Brielle is mine.*

Just as I was about to pump a celebratory fist in the air over locking Bree down, the music lowered, and Zanaé said, "When I look sexy, I sound sexy."

"Damn," I muttered in awe and was promptly pinched by Brielle. "What?" I asked, feigning innocence.

She rolled her eyes as a woman I didn't recognize entered the booth to chat with Zanaé.

"I love you, but I'm not blind," I said offhandedly. Bree turned her entire body to face me. "What?" I asked again, genuinely confused about what I'd done now. If Bree wanted me to pretend the woman wasn't fine, I was whipped enough to go along with it.

"You love me, Walter?"

My lip curled up toward my nose as I weighed whether to come right out with it. I hadn't scared her off this far. "I've loved you since forever," I tried, and leaned down and kissed her cheek, not concerned that we weren't alone.

"Romantically?"

"Yes." I hadn't intended to express my feelings for Brielle on yet another work trip, but my word vomit had shown my hand. The shocking part was now that it was out in the open, I was good with her knowing.

"Since when?"

The fire in Brielle's slanted eyes had my heart and my dick on one accord. Both tightened in response to her energy.

"Since I saw your makeover. I'd loved you and found you attractive long before then, but seeing you come alive in front of my eyes made something inside of me snap. At first, I was ashamed that I was thirsting over my best friend, then I was pissed at anybody who had the nerve to shoot their shot at you." I got heated just thinking about it.

"And then?"

A wide grin covered my face. "And then I was ready to do whatever it took to be your hall pass." I closed my eyes at the joyous memory. I leaned down and whispered beside her ear, "Once I put my face between your thighs, I was committed to moving heaven and earth to make you mine."

Now it was her turn to shudder with memories of our time together. Part of me was anxious to get at her again, and another part of me was confident we had the rest of our lives to be together. She lifted and planted a sensuous kiss on my lips.

"Can y'all stop being this cute?" a small, raspy voice rang out behind us. I whipped around like I'd been caught with my hands in the cookie jar. With an even bigger smile on my face, I pulled Brielle into my side and faced the tiny icon.

"This song..." Bree gushed.

"Ron tried to warn you. He was right as usual. I couldn't resist. Do you like it?" Zanaé was nervous as she awaited our response.

I piped up. "It's the dopest shit ever, and the fact that it's about to be played repeatedly for the ad is icing on the cake."

Zanaé's lips curled into a hopeful smile. "Your girl isn't the only creative one in the room, OK."

The three of us fell out in laughter over the understatement of the century but were only given several minutes together before Zanaé was once again whisked away.

"Thank you again for making time to get here so quickly," she said as she walked backward in another direction.

"Are you kidding? Thank you for giving us the five-star treatment," Bree returned.

Zanaé turned to leave us but then whipped around to face us once again. "Promise me one thing."

"Done," I said with my head in my phone. I was promptly elbowed by my equally jealous woman.

I lifted my head in time to see Zanaé's smirk at our playfight when she added, "Invite me to the wedding."

"Done," Bree said this time as I stiffened.

WE TALKED about the ad and Zanaé's estate on the way back to the resort. Bree went on and on about how she couldn't wait to take London to the pool, but all I could focus on was the word wedding. Bree had known me long enough to know I didn't believe in the institution of marriage. Then again, I was fully aware that she did. How the hell would we handle our conflicting outlooks on a topic as significant as getting married?

As we made our way to our adjoined rooms, I asked Bree if she was fine if I took a much-needed nap while she spent time with London and our friends.

"Are you OK, baby?" she purred. The resonance of her sweet tone tickled my ears and threatened to wake up my dick when she spoke.

I nodded, hopeful she wouldn't pick up on my trepidation. She regarded me for long moments, and instead of using words, Brielle stood on her tiptoes and placed a loving kiss on my lips. When she pulled away, I was left with remnants of cherry flavored lipstick on my mouth. *Damn she tastes good.*

"Call me later?"

I hugged and kissed her again as if to ease her concern. "Yup."

Bree

MY TIME WITH LONDON, Chanté, Chase, and Hakeem at the pool was beyond satisfying. I couldn't remember the last time I had anything remotely close to a family vacation. Walter avoided me because of my response to Zanaé, but what the hell did he expect me to say to her request for an invite? It wasn't any of her business what we did after we left, but it seemed like the right thing to do to allow her to get her hopes up. What harm would it do?

I'd gotten London dinner and laid him down to sleep for the night. Chanté offered to have him sleep in her room, but I filled her in on Walter's mood and how I wouldn't need her assistance for the evening. She frowned but let it go since we had two more nights and were honestly spent from the day's events.

With the baby cam aimed at my sonshine and the monitor positioned inside of the bathroom, I went about the business of my evening routine. After I was satisfied with my shower and skincare, I snapped a picture of myself in the sleepwear I bought specifically for this trip. I texted it to Walt without any words, deciding if he needed his space, I wouldn't press it. I drifted off without a response from him.

I was in a deep sleep when the glow of my phone pulled me from my restful state. It was an alert that The Lone Wolf posted another blog. Hopeful I'd get some insight into Dizzy's current headspace, I clicked on the article entitled, *"When she wants, 'I do', but he don't."*

I held my breath as the title knocked the wind out of me.

Is there ever a circumstance where a man genuinely loves a woman from the depths of his soul and still doesn't want marriage? Is there an acceptable reason for women? I doubt it. Because of the oversaturation of excuses from the male species to avoid a commitment, we all get grouped into one not-shit community.

If you've read my blog long enough, you know my stance on the institution of marriage. It's straight up trash and wasn't designed with the descendants of enslaved Africans in mind. I can see a lot of you rolling your eyes and throwing me back to the Hotep hills from whence I came but hear me out. I fucked around and fell in love. Not a little bit, but I fuck with my girl heavy. I would walk through hell with gasoline draws on just to give her a glass of water. Anything she wants, I'll do it. Anything her son needs, I'll provide it. The only area I seem to fall short is marriage.

Can I commit to her without involving the state? Can't I provide for her financially without a legal ceremony? I'll move her into my house and pay both of our bills if she wants. I'll build her a brand-new house if she asks me to. Isn't that enough? I admit a huge part of me is being selfish. I've known this woman for damn near two decades, so I know all too well how important marriage is to her. If I wasn't interested, I should have chosen someone who was on the same page, but my heart had other plans. Usually, I have the answer to the questions I pose. In this instance I really want to know, what the hell do I do if she wants 'I do', but I don't?

My cheeks were wet as I held onto Dizzy's every word. The consideration he had for me while being brutally honest about what he wanted was overwhelming. He may have been conflicted about our different beliefs, but I was fully assured. Walter loved me like I deserved, and after everything I'd been through with Lance's trifling ass, marriage was no longer a deal breaker for me. That was how much I loved the man in the room next to mine.

I sniffled as I exited the blog and navigated to my text messages.

ME:

Can I come over?

I had no idea when Walter had posted the blog. It was possible it went live immediately, but maybe he'd gone to sleep or ventured out to explore the resort to clear his mind. I didn't have much time to ruminate, because his response came through within seconds.

MY WALT DIZZY:

Where's London?

ME:

I have the monitor and can keep an eye on him with it

MY WALT DIZZY:

You sure he'll be alright?

ME:

Yes, baby

The sound of the heavy lock turning at our adjoined doors startled me. I opened my side and found him leaning against the doorframe. The only clothing he wore was a pair of thin pajama pants that hung low on his hips putting both his toned inguinal creases on display and making my mouth water. His locs were free and framed his handsome face like a mane.

"Hey," I said. Although I was painstakingly turned on by him, my eyes began to water at the thought of the words he'd written for me.

"Don't cry, baby." Walter pulled me into him. His fresh scent tickled my nose when he did.

I genuinely hadn't meant to allow my emotions to get the best of me, but given the circumstances, I couldn't help it. "You would walk through hell with gasoline drawers on for me?" I quipped.

He leaned down and peered into my eyes. Without a hint of laughter, he responded, "Hell yeah."

"Brielle, I'm sorry for acting strange after Zanaé's comment about a wedding. It's just—"

I lifted onto my tiptoes and pressed my lips against him, smothering his words. The fact that he was willing to apologize to me was wild. He'd told Blueface and Chrisean's internet that he loved me *and* my son. Walter wanted to build with me. He was already more of a husband than the fake one I thought I married.

Would I ultimately want to be Mrs. Simmons? Absolutely, but for him, I was willing to find a middle ground... whatever that was.

Walter tugged me toward him by my waist and gently shut my side of the door. He separated from me, leaving me whining, when he retrieved the monitor from my hand and smiled down at London. He propped it on a nearby table and aimed the screen in our direction. I sauntered over to where he placed it and turned it around. He sucked in a ragged breath when he caught a glimpse of my backside.

"He doesn't need to see this," I purred.

"Uh, OK. What you got on, Bree?"

I slowly turned back to face the beautiful, complex man before me. "You like it?"

His hooded eyes were trained on me as I took the two steps to re-enter his space. In place of words, he nodded.

"I wanna show you how much you mean to me," I continued while I led him to a nearby couch.

Walter's body tightened when I lightly pushed him so he was seated, bringing his face eye level to the area where my thighs met. His lust-filled eyes were set low, and I couldn't wait to get my hands on him. I was determined to utilize every trick I'd learned from an online sensation who swore she gave the best head and hand jobs. She made an entire series dedicated to showing other women how to make their man's toes curl.

One of the points she pressed was to keep eye contact, which wasn't a problem for me, because Walter Dizzy Simmons was so damn fine. I lowered to my knees in front of him and easily freed his dick from his pajamas. I ran my hands down his muscular body, then licked my hands until they were nice and slick. Walter rested his head on the back of the couch with pure adoration in his eyes as he watched me.

With a moistened hand, I grabbed his shaft and leaned forward to lick and suck the head of his dick where the woman insisted was his most sensitive spot. The moan that slipped from Dizzy's mouth was confirmation that sis hadn't lied. I twirled my tongue around the area, stopping only to give some attention to the slit where his children would eventually make their way down my throat. All the while, I kept a tight grip on his shaft and my eyes on him. I tugged on his dick in a way I initially thought would hurt him, but I learned that men gripped their meat much harder than women did, so there was no reason for me to be gentle.

"Shit, Brielle."

Walter hadn't seen anything because I'd just gotten started. I tugged on him, and I teased the head with my tongue. I used a two-hand method and stroked him until his eyes rolled back. I was in a powerful position, and it was one of the most exhilarating feelings. When my hands grew tired from the churning butter motion I employed, I released him and continued my oral escapade with no hands.

I ran my tongue along the most prominent vein I saw. That was when it happened. The strong man beneath me squealed, and his toes contorted like they were doing sign language. I covered him with my warm mouth and relaxed my throat. I wasn't a professional at the art of deep throating, but I was willing to practice until I made him feel the way I felt because of the way he loved me.

Somehow, Walter's already substantial dick grew in my mouth. I breathed through my nose with his tip massaging my uvula, determined not to tap out. I let saliva coat him while I covered my teeth and slowly moved up and down his length.

"Fuck!"

It was when my hand gently cupped his balls that he grasped me by my arms and lifted me to face him.

"What are you doing to me, baby?"

"Making you feel as good as you make me feel, Dizzy," I replied honestly. "And I wasn't finished."

He shuddered. "What's gotten into you? You're down there acting like my own personal head doctor."

The corners of my mouth lifted. He'd given me the highest compliment. I got distracted by the sight of the engorged monster between his legs. The veins were now more pronounced, and I drooled just seeing it at attention.

"Don't even try it. You're done."

"Why?" I whined in protest.

His eyebrows bunched, and his face twisted. "Because I'll fuck around and not let you see the light of day if you keep it up," he threatened.

My smirk deepened as he pulled me on top of him. I settled down onto his lap, and the lines in his face deepened. Walter's grumpy face and sexually satisfied face were practically indistinguishable. A gush of moisture gathered between my legs making for a highly slippery ride. I grinded my center against his and bit into my bottom lip as his mouth formed a silent O.

His strong hands gripped my breasts as if he'd just remembered he could use them. Walter leaned forward and devoured the right one while he used his nimble fingers to titillate my left nipple.

"What happened?" He whined when he lifted his head to marvel at me.

"Huh?" I asked as I continued to move my hips in a wavelike motion that extended to the deep arch in my back.

"It was good the first time, but it wasn't this damn salacious," he moaned.

I leaned forward with my large breasts pressed against his hard chest and brought my lips next to his ear. "That was before I read how you felt about me."

"Shit! I thought you would be pissed the moment you saw the title. Fuck!"

He cussed my ass out because I flicked his earlobe with my tongue. This side of me had been suppressed without someone safe to go there with. Walter was perfect, from his immaculate body to the unwavering way he cared for me.

"I gotta see this ass from behind," he cried out.

"Are you sure about that?"

"Got dammit, Bree." He stood with me still on his lap. My legs automatically wrapped around his waist. Walter kissed me in a way that had me convinced I'd be satisfied for the rest of my life. He walked me away from the couch and gently brought me to my feet. I was barely on the ground for two seconds before he lightly tossed me on the bed.

A satisfied grin covered my face when I looked up at him. A guttural groan rumbled deep within Walter's throat, causing yet another gush of moisture to trickle down my thigh.

"Turn around, baby."

I did as I was asked. Walter entered me smoothly. He moved his hips in a slow grind that had me on the verge of an orgasm. I'd been so focused on pleasing him that the moment I was on the receiving end, my body responded immediately.

"Cum for me, Bree."

Why the hell did he have to go and say that. As if he had the ability to call my release into existence, my walls tightened around him.

"Dizzy!" I squealed.

"Yeah, baby. Cum for me." He kept the same methodical pace as he slid in and out of my drenched pussy.

"Please," I whined.

"Please, what?"

"Fuck me, daddy."

"No."

I craned my head back to see a genuine smile on his sexy face.

"Why?" I hummed.

"I need to make love to you," was Walter's response. He said the words while he continued his original, unhurried pace, and it was my undoing.

My back arched, and I gripped the sheets while wave after wave of pleasure coursed through my body. I unraveled in front of him, only to hear his warning.

"I'm about to cum, baby," he said as his strokes went deeper. How he maintained the same momentum was beyond me.

My body continued to vibrate as Walter slammed into me a few more times before reaching his own peak.

"Damn, I love you," he said as he turned us on our sides with our satiated bodies still joined.

thirteen

Walter

IT WAS THE LAST DAY OF OUR WORK TRIP, AND WE WERE AT a well-known restaurant—courtesy of Zanaé—before we were set to return home. All I could think about was how deeply I'd fallen in love with my best friend. Brielle was an amazing woman and mother with a pussy I'd go to war for.

The more time I thought about it, the more I was willing to adjust my outlook on marriage. I still didn't agree with involving a corrupt government in my relationship, but what if something happened to me? I'd want Bree and London to be taken care of.

Giving her my last name would make all that much easier. My highest priority was their safety and happiness. Marriage would provide both of those for Bree. Not only was she worth it, but her head game was enough to have me rethink my entire life. A shiver ran up my spine at the thought of what she'd done to me the night before.

Her hand lightly brushed against my arm, making my body

react. I cleared my throat as she leaned in and asked, "Are you OK, Walter?"

Her sensual voice hadn't helped matters. My eyes fell to those same lips that kissed and sucked my dick like a pro hours earlier. I cleared my throat again.

"I'm good."

"Flashbacks," Chanté teased from across the table.

She and Chase wore matching grins as they elbowed each other, making fun of me. I shrugged, unwilling to deny it. Once again, my mind drifted from our conversation as Bree fed London and filled our friends in on our time with Zanaé.

There was a different level of pressure involved with returning to McHaven this time around. For one, Lance was no longer a factor in whether Bree and I could be together. In the depth of my soul, I was committed to being with her for the rest of my life. How could I communicate that to her without compromising my beliefs? Did I still think marriage was a waste now that I was madly in love?

Those questions ran through my mind as Chase and I were assured our bill had already been taken care of. The internal interrogation didn't quiet on the ride to the airport, nor did my spirit settle on our private flight home. When I walked Brielle and London to the door, he leaned in for me to pick him up. I willingly accepted his squishy body and almost passed out when he said, "Love Diz." He went on to put his chubby hand over his mouth as if to blow me a kiss.

I looked down at Bree to confirm I hadn't hallucinated. Her wide smile and the sparkle in her eyes were all the validation I needed.

"Stay with us," she purred.

"OK."

I hustled to the car that had dropped Chanté, Chase, and Hakeem off first to retrieve my belongings. I tipped him and sent him on his way. I ran back to her front door, then steadied my breath before I entered. I'd been in Brielle's home more times than I could count, and generally, I was comfortable here. Now though, it was glaringly obvious that the woman who held my heart had shared this space with a man I didn't want to be reminded of. The family pictures haunted me as I parked myself on the sofa in the living room.

While Bree got London changed and put him down for a nap, I read some of the comments to my last blog.

One user commented, *"Whoever she is is lucky as hell. I know you're anonymous, but I can tell you're fine as hell. Then, you got the nerve to be out loud with your love for her. Maybe y'all could do a non-official ceremony as a middle ground. She may need more assurance than your words that you're not fucking around and that you're going to stick around, especially if she has a child."*

Another person said, *"He probably runs this game on every woman he meets and is looking for a good enough excuse to throw at them when the woman presses him for answers."*

One of the few male comments read, *"If you've known her for fifteen years then she also knows your views on marriage. Why should you change and she gets what she wants?"*

I liked the first response where the person mentioned Bree may want more than just my words. It was the last comment that made my eyes bulge.

*"You are more important to me than marriage, Dizzy. You're my best friend turned lover. I respect your outlook on the institution more than you know. We've been in each other's lives for years and that's definitely not going to change now that I know what that mouth do. *crying laughing emoji. Your commitment to me is stronger than any example I've seen. I don't need 'I do', all I need is you. I love you, BKB.*

My eyes were glassy as I read Brielle's words repeatedly. Many women replied under Bree's comment, congratulating her and me.

She had hundreds of likes and only a few warnings to watch out for me.

"Hey," she said softly.

I gazed up to find her furrowed brows locked in on me. She was stunning. The sweatsuit she wore wasn't overly sensual, but it still hugged her body in a way that made my mouth water. I pulled her to sit on my lap as I aimed my phone in her direction. The lines in her forehead relaxed and were replaced with an endearing smile.

She angled her head back to kiss me, and I gladly accepted it.

"Is London napping?"

She pointed at the monitor to confirm he was.

She yawned which earned her a throaty laugh from me. I was also tired from our day of travel. I shifted her off my lap and leaned back, positioning her in front of me on her couch as I kissed the back of her neck.

"I love what you wrote, Bree."

"I wrote it because I love you, Dizzy."

"I love you too."

Bree

I WAS OFFICIALLY in a new rhythm. We'd been back from our second Zanaé trip for almost three weeks. Exhausted, unhappy Bree had been replaced with a well-rested, glowing version of myself. Walter insisted that he wouldn't sit by while I did everything. His first order of business was that I only dropped off and picked London up from school a few times a week. The other days were Lance's responsibility.

He wanted me to move out of my house and move in with him permanently, but I wasn't quite ready. It was one thing to be tasked with processing the fact that I'd never legally been married and a whole other thing to move in with Walter without something concrete. Walter had shown me no reason to doubt his loyalty to me and London, but it didn't seem wise to uproot us with no real plan or way for me to protect myself. I didn't want to jump from one toxic situation to an unstable one.

Despite my internal unrest, Walter had demonstrated his commitment to me in every way that mattered. He'd set up a play area for London in his home and cleared out a bedroom for him for the nights we stayed over. It was the most thoughtful gesture. On the nights I was exhausted from work, he would keep London occupied with toddler puzzles while he played with him or worked on his own alongside him.

London was comfortable in Walter's space. These days he seemed to prefer it over the few days we were at home, for one reason or another. It was Saturday and I was spent. I was plopped on Walter's oversized couch with my laptop opened. Walter took a seat beside me with the baby monitor in his hand.

"He made me read him three books," he fussed.

London was fast asleep in the three-in-one crib Walter bought him.

"He loves it here," I admitted.

"I love him here too." Walter sat on the opposite end and motioned for me to close my work. I did and willingly gave him my feet.

"My mom is itching to come and see London," he said as his thumb pressed into the sole of my foot, earning him a moan from me.

My eyes popped open. "Mama Grace knows I'm practically living here?"

He nodded. "And she can't believe I had the nerve to keep you from her."

"Invite her over or we could go there. Either is fine," I insisted.

Grace was such a phenomenal woman and mother. I called her from time to time to get her opinion on London's milestones. I'd been ashamed to reach out now that I was no longer married and was letting her son do unspeakable acts to me. My cheeks heated at the thought.

"She already knows," he said as his fingers continued their work.

I lifted from my relaxed position on the couch. "She knows what?"

"That I'm fucking you every chance I get," he said matter-of-factly. "I'm kidding. I didn't tell her, but she knows that too. She said I hadn't been in a grouchy mood in weeks. I explained everything about Lance and how our relationship has evolved past friends."

"What did she say?" I asked with my bottom lip tucked between my teeth. I was closer to Grace than my own mother. Her opinion meant a lot to me.

"She said it was about time," he responded with a smirk. "I guess she always thought we should get together."

Walter released my foot and shifted to settle between my legs. I opened them for him without hesitation. I'd been turned on by the way he took care of my son but scolded myself for my dirty thoughts. He pressed his lips to mine, making the moisture gathered between my legs gush. Walter slipped his hand down the front of my pants and hissed when his fingers swiped against my center.

"You're so fucking wet, Bree," he groaned.

"It's your fault," I purred.

He'd slipped my pants below my hips when a light knock sounded at his front door.

"Fuck," he said into the couch.

I ran my tongue alongside his ear and whispered, "We have all night, baby."

"You're not helping." He fussed as he lifted and adjusted himself while I watched. "Freaky ass woman."

I grabbed the monitor, relieved that London was still napping. Once he fell asleep, the chances of him being awakened before the end of his nap were low, but I kept an eye out just in case.

"Uh, hey," Walter said.

"Can we talk?" Melina pleaded.

Hell, no! What was she doing here? Walter said they'd broken things off the night after I found Lance with Emma. I rolled my eyes just thinking about how awful things were for me at that time.

"Uh, this is not a good time," Walter tried.

"You already got another bitch in here?" she pressed.

I wasn't surprised at her reaction. Walter was a certified sex god. He was skilled in the art of pleasing women. The thought of him moving on with someone else was enough to drive any woman insane.

"Melina, keep your voice down," he whisper-yelled.

There was a scuffle at the door, and before I could leave the living room, Melina stood face to face with me, wearing a scowl on her captivating face. She gave me a once over as I absentmindedly used my hand to smooth down the curls of my 'fro.

"You swore up and down that she was your best friend. You're fucking her?" she demanded of Walter, although she hadn't moved her eyes from me.

Walter grabbed her by the waist and pulled her away from me. "First of all, keep your voice down. And second, she was my best friend."

"Was?" Tears streamed her beautiful cheeks, and I wanted to disappear. She wasn't right for Walter, but I could only imagine how she must have felt seeing us together after all the times he reassured her there was nothing between us.

"Let's talk outside," Walter said firmly, but gently.

Rage covered her features, and her fists were clenched beside her, but she relented. I released a ragged breath once the two of them were outside.

Walt

I SLOWLY REENTERED my house after I finally convinced Melina to leave. She was furious to find me with Bree after I'd sworn we were friends the entire time Melina and I dated. I was honest about Bree's and my timeline. It turned out Melina only wanted to talk because she'd started dating someone at M3 and wanted to be the one to tell me. She admitted she lost her cool at the thought that I moved on, only to find out the woman was Brielle.

I prayed Brielle wasn't pissed with me and that she wouldn't withhold her magical pussy. There was no one else in the world I wanted. I'd barely made it into the living room when she attacked me with sloppy kisses.

"Shit!"

She dropped to her knees before me and freed me from my sweats.

"Brielle, what are you doing?" I grunted as she covered me with her warm mouth.

"Reminding you who you belong to," she said, popping me out and back into her mouth.

"Fuck."

Bree got better every time she gave me head, and each time, I was baffled by how that was possible. My eyes were squeezed shut as she hummed on my dick. Sensations vibrated through me as the woman I loved let loud sucking sounds escape her mouth. Spit covered me and dripped down onto the floor. It was when she slipped me out of her mouth and gently sucked my balls that I temporarily went deaf.

"Baby," I crooned.

When I did find the strength to open my eyes and peek down at her, Bree's eyes were locked on mine. She used two hands to massage my dick and flicked her tongue around the head.

"I'm about to cum, baby." I attempted to step back but was held in place by Brielle's surprisingly strong grip, or maybe I was just too weak to move. She let my seed shoot down her throat. My knees buckled, and I had to hold the wall to steady myself. She flicked her tongue around my super-sensitive, now semi-erect dick.

"Why?" was all I could manage to ask as I wiggled out of her grasp.

She stood and brought her beautiful mouth to mine. "Because I love you, and I want you to know who you belong to." She hadn't broken eye contact, and a shiver ran the length of my spine. Melina wasn't safe if she showed up at my house again. By the fierce look in her eyes, Bree would lay hands next time.

"And you belong to me too," I muttered.

"Well," she teased as she waved her hand back and forth as if to say maybe.

"You're not the only territorial one, Bree," I said as I pulled her ass toward me.

"Good."

BREE and I dropped London Bridges off at daycare together. Some of the women were a little too friendly with me, but I was grateful to see how much they loved my guy. He'd grown on me the more time they spent at my house. Bree had it covered, but I was still immensely protective of him. He already had a father, but I wanted to be in his life however he and Bree would have me.

As I drove us to M3, I said, "I'm surprised you put me on the approved pick-up list."

She shrugged. "It just makes sense. If anything happened, I would hate for them to refuse to release London to you since we all live together."

I almost wrecked.

"What's wrong with you, Walter?" she asked with wide eyes.

I stole a glance in her direction. "You live with me?"

Her mouth dropped open, but she didn't say a word.

"And you must be trying to make me late by doing your mouth like that."

Bree made my head spin. It didn't matter how many times I had her, I wanted her just as badly.

"I want nothing more than to move out of my house. I guess I've been afraid to be all in. What if..."

"What if what? Talk to me, baby."

We were parked in the M3 garage as I rested my hand on her thigh. She squirmed in the passenger seat. With a smirk on my face, I added, "I'm serious. Tell me why you're afraid."

"I gave my ex so many chances because I was taught that's what you do, even though he played in my face repeatedly. With you, we aren't traditional—"

"About that," I cut in.

"It's OK, Dizzy. We're not traditional, but you've shown me you can be trusted with my heart and my son. I don't take that lightly. I respect you, I admire you, and I love you."

A lump formed in my throat as I allowed her words to wash over me.

"Walter."

"Yeah, baby."

"Can I have a little more time?"

We stared at each other for long moments like the practice of eye gazing. We didn't use words, but our communication continued. When Aiden hustled past, tripping when he saw us together, we burst into laughter.

"Yes. Take all the time you need."

Bree

WALTER COULDN'T KEEP his eyes off me. I'd dressed up, but he'd seen me get ready. None of that was enough to keep him from watching my every move. Joi and Aiden weren't the only ones to notice. A few female coworkers gave me wide smiles as they complimented me and pointed out my new glow.

The department was gathered in the conference room for an unscheduled meeting with Joi. I had the bright idea to sit across from Walter so he'd keep his hands off me. The distance helped with touching, but only amplified the lustful glances he threw my way, even while we were in conversation with other people.

"This won't be long," Joi said as she made her way to the front. She lowered the lights and announced, "Here is the *CocoaKiss Cosmetics* campaign set to air this afternoon."

The moment the commercial started, there were gasps from our coworkers as they stared in disbelief. I could barely swallow as I watched Walter lean down and place a sweet kiss to my cheek. It was footage from the day of the shoot. The next second, I leaned up on my tiptoes and kissed his lips after he just admitted he loved me.

Water crowded my eyes as the music for Zanaé's new track filtered through the speakers. The bass made some of the M3 employees bounce in their seats. Zanaé finally came into focus just in time for her to sing the lyrics about her justified hall pass. Another shot of Walter with me pulled into his side and a huge grin on his face was placed in the ad in time with the lyrics, making my cheeks heat.

Joi glared at me, and I prayed I wouldn't need to find a new job. There was no denying what Aiden had undoubtedly already told her. The music lowered as the commercial cut to Zanaé in the studio. She applied the product then said the line Walter and I came up with. "When I look sexy, I sound sexy." It ended with a close-up of the product next to a QR code for purchase.

The room erupted into applause. The commercial was just about a minute, but that sixty seconds packed a powerful punch. Zanaé plugged her song, the brand, and Walter's and my relationship. I tore my eyes from the blank screen in time to see Walt's eyes on me. My mouth watered, and my center pulsed under his intense gaze.

He mouthed, "I love you," earning more hoots and whistles from our coworkers.

"You lucky bitch," Samantha whispered as she shook my arm. She was usually a quiet woman who buried herself in numbers, but even she couldn't deny the chemistry between us. I was so overwhelmed with how well the ad turned out and with Walter's loud expression of love for me that I hadn't realized he was beside my chair until he cleared his throat.

He wet his lips and reached his hand out for me as he announced, "Bree and I need to make an appointment with HR."

There were more gasps as I stood. I peered over at Joi, who gave her blessing by nodding toward the door. *Thank God.*

Walter closed the door and walked me backward against a wall away from the conference room.

"Don't we need to tell HR about our relationship?" I whispered.

"I emailed them this morning and was assured all they needed was an acknowledgment. They'll send us forms to sign later. I just needed to get you alone. Did you see how fine you looked in that commercial and how fat your ass was in them tight pants?" he moaned.

I smirked up at him just as he grabbed both sides of my face and kissed me feverishly.

"Your place or mine?" he asked with a mischievous grin on his face.

Walt

WE ENDED up going back to my place after I whisked Bree from work because although Lance was a nonfactor, I couldn't bring myself to fuck her in their house. I hung out with her and London there, but that was as far as it went. We were at her house now because she wanted to pack a few more things. I was more than ready for her to move in with me for good, but I'd agreed to be as patient with her as she'd been with me.

Bree waved at a man I didn't recognize as we made our way back to the car. I held London Bridges who did his best to slip from my arms.

"I'll let you down as soon as we're in the grass, little man," I assured him. "Who is that, baby?" I asked as Bree stood watching London and me.

She shrugged. "I've seen him a couple times. He lives across the street."

I touched my lip to the tip of my nose as I stared at the stranger unashamed. Something was off about him, and since Bree and London occasionally stayed here alone, my gut was unsettled, not knowing who was in her neighborhood.

"Did you see a move-in truck?"

Bree grabbed London from me and placed a kiss on my lips. "You're overreacting. It's almost time for London's nap," she sang.

My eyebrows shot up, and my pants tightened. The run in with her neighbor still didn't sit right with me, but I would deal with it after I drove us to my house and dealt with Brielle. She could have me any time she wanted, and she'd just given me a not-so-subtle hint that she was ready... again. The sooner we got out of there the sooner I could do something about it.

fourteen

Bree

Awkward was an understatement for the tension in the air at Walter's house. He'd invited Grace over to see London, and after about twenty minutes, Mason showed up. We were in the room off the kitchen that Walter designated as London's playroom. London waved and said, "Hi" to Mason from Grace's lap. Each time Mason smiled at him, he hid his face in Grace's chest only to turn around and do it again.

Mason cleared his throat. "This is a cute kid, Brielle," he offered.

"Remember when Walter was this age?" Grace muttered.

"He was a damn handful." Mason chuckled. "Still is."

London toddled in Mason's direction and leaned forward until he picked him up. "Happy now?" Mason asked. London drooled and nodded his head.

I could appreciate where Walter got his cantankerous temperament. I'd never had the pleasure of being around Mason for an extended period.

"Sorry about that," I offered as I used London's bib to wipe his face. "I don't know why he drools so much. He should be done with it by now."

"Does he get fussy when he gets a tooth?" Grace queried.

"Actually, he doesn't. He'll just open his mouth and boom another one," I said in my DJ Khalid voice.

Grace grabbed for London again, and he went willingly. "Babies who have a lot of saliva usually don't complain when their teeth come through. I know it seems like a nuisance, but it's really a blessing."

My heart smiled. Walter may have been uncomfortable with his estranged parents in the same place, but I experienced nothing but love radiating from the two of them. My parents had been married for decades, but I wouldn't characterize what they shared as love. Walter leaned in and placed a quick kiss to my cheek, then rested his arm around me while we sat and watched his parents on the ground with London.

"It's none of my business, but is London's father OK with Walter's involvement with you and this beautiful child?" Mason asked with his eyes still on London.

"You're right. It's none of your business," Walter responded flatly, then stood. "Let me talk to you in the next room, Pop."

Walter always referred to his dad as Mason, so maybe they'd had a civil conversation before today. I had no idea what that was like. As if I spoke my own parents up, my phone vibrated with a text from my parental units.

DAD:

Come to the house, now!

ME:

Is everything OK?

He didn't respond to my text. I was able to calm my fear that someone was hurt simply by recalling all the times my mom and dad sent these urgent messages only to ask a question that could have been written out or expressed over the phone. The bottom line was that they were extra as hell—dramatic for no reason.

"What is it, Brielle?" Grace asked as London twirled her hoop earrings.

"It's my father."

"Is he OK, dear?" she asked in a concerned tone. Grace's support was foreign in my world, but I appreciated it more than she knew.

"I'm not sure. He wants me to come home."

As if I'd called his name, or he sensed my distress, Walter reentered the playroom with his father on his heels. They both wore matching mean mugs with a slight grin that I couldn't wait to ask Walter about. In the past, I'd joke about how fine Mason was and insisted I could give Grace a run for her money. Walter's dad was an older, seasoned version of his only child. It had been harmless when we were best friends but was no longer appropriate, given our change in status.

I scolded myself and promptly averted my gaze from my man's daddy.

Sitting back down beside me, Dizzy asked, "What happened?"

I showed him the screen of my phone, and his frown deepened. "You want me to go with you?"

I nodded. I'd never had emotional support with Lance—or any other support for that matter. It was a relief not to have to walk through my parents' door alone.

"It was nice to meet you, London, and it was a pleasure seeing you again, Brielle," Mason said with the same sparkle he had since he and Walter finished their chat. London waved his chunky hand and blew a kiss in his direction.

"Don't let this be the last time I see him," Grace said as she pressed her cheek against London's. "He's so precious."

"I won't. I promise."

Walt

I THOUGHT my family was dysfunctional, but the Barnes family took toxic to a whole other level. It reminded me that my parents weren't so bad. Once I explained to Mason about Lance and told him I'd do whatever it took to keep Bree safe and happy, including marry her, he teared up. He told me he was proud of me, and we shared a moment I didn't think I would in my adult life.

I owed that to Brielle. She'd elevated my life in a way I never thought was possible. My father and I had a long road ahead of us, but I was pleased with where we were currently.

As soon as my lady's sexy toes stepped over the threshold, her people went in.

"Can you explain this?" her mom, Erica, asked as she pointed toward the paused Zanaé *CocoaKiss Cosmetics* campaign.

I smiled. I'd only seen it once, and Brielle's ass on national television did something to me. Her brother, Trevor, mugged me and took London from my arms.

"Does Lance know you got your boyfriend around my nephew?" Trevor barked in a tone that was too intense for a woman who happened to be his sister.

"I didn't raise you like this!" Her father, Timothy, thundered.

I stepped up. "This is not what it looks like," I reasoned.

"So, you're not kissing a married woman in this commercial?" her father asked sarcastically. He was heavily involved in the church, but his glare was as deadly as any other man who would go to bat for their daughter.

"No, sir," I answered confidently.

Trevor laughed, causing London to jump.

He was lucky Bree's mother took him before I could.

"That's you, ain't it, Walter?" Timothy asked incredulously.

I peered down at Brielle who appeared to have lost her voice. "You want me to address this?" I asked.

She nodded and accepted the hand I offered. "Bree ain't married."

"You's a got damn lie," her brother spat.

His parents glared at him but quickly returned their focus to me. "Your wife didn't tell you that your son-in-law's name is not Lance?"

The older man's head shot in his wife's direction.

"He's got a criminal background and lied about it on their wedding certificate, making the marriage null and constituting marriage fraud. He also cheated on Brielle," I continued.

"We all have fallen short—"

"I know you are not about to fix your lips to excuse what buddy did to your daughter," I said, exhausted and quite frankly disappointed that Bree had to deal with this type of treatment from her family.

"All these years, Brielle has insisted the two of you were just friends." He tried taking another angle, because what they weren't going to do was pretend Bree deserved bad behavior in the name of religion.

"Daddy, we were just friends... until recently," she said as she smiled up at me.

"Fornicating friends?" her father asked, even though it was none of his damn business.

"Daddy!" Bree tried.

Timothy marched in my direction, needing to tilt his head up to face me. I released Brielle with my eyes locked on his.

"Do you plan on making an honest woman of my daughter?"

Without hesitation, I responded, "Yes, sir."

"I know you, Walter. For years, you've been coming in and out of here professing that you don't believe in anything—not marriage, religion, or school."

Trevor kissed his teeth.

"How exactly are you going to show up for her any differently than you claim Lance has?"

I swallowed. I didn't owe this man shit, but since he was her father, on some level, Bree still craved his validation and wanted his approval. "First of all, there's not a woman in the world who could take my attention away from your daughter. I've had a crush on Zanaé for years, and I couldn't tell you what she looked like in person because I barely noticed her."

"Now I know your ass is lying." Trevor sneered.

"Hush, boy," Erica spat.

My eyes fell to Bree, who wore a blush.

"I've loved your daughter as a friend for fifteen years. Now that we've become more, there's nothing I wouldn't do to ensure she and London are happy and well taken care of."

My eyes swung over to Erica to find that they were glassy. She motioned for Bree to come closer, and I was on high alert. When she leaned forward and hugged Brielle, I released a sigh of relief. "I'm not going to hurt her," Erica teased. "I'm sorry, Bree Baby," her mother said, shocking us both.

"Huh?" Trevor shrieked.

"What?" Timothy inserted.

"Don't act so surprised. Have you been listening to this man speak? He's been more of a husband to Brielle, in the small amount of time they've been an item, than Lance ever was."

"Mama," Trevor tried.

"Your loyalty to Lance has nothing to do with your sister," her mother fussed.

I did a terrible job holding in my chuckle, but cleared my throat when her father shot me a steely look. "You plan to marry Brielle?" her father asked.

"I'll do whatever it takes to keep her safe and make her happy. The more time I spend thinking about it, the more I realize marriage will do both."

"No, it won't," Bree started as she moved back in my direction. "You already make me happy, Dizzy, and getting married definitely didn't keep me safe the first time."

"If something happens to me, I want to make sure you and London don't have to worry about money, and I know how important marriage is to you. I love you more than I don't believe in it, Bree Bree," I said, hoping I could convince her how deeply I loved her.

"You'll never guess what's happening at the house," Trevor said into his phone. "Bree broke up with Lance for her water head ass friend."

"TT, who are you talking to?" Bree's mother asked with her eyebrows furrowed.

"Dustin," he said as he left the room.

"Are you serious?" Bree asked.

I nodded. "I'll do whatever you want, willingly!"

She smirked at me, and I couldn't help myself when I leaned down and placed a kiss on her mouth.

London blew a kiss, melting my heart. I grabbed him with her mother's permission and redirected my attention to her father. "Is that alright with you, sir?"

Timothy rubbed a hand down the back of his head. "Does it matter?" he asked Bree.

She shook her head. "Not really, but it would make things easier if you did."

Instead of responding, he pulled Bree into a side hug and whispered, "I'm sorry I didn't interject when you weren't happy with Lance. Seeing how your friend…" he amended his words when Bree stiffened. "Seeing how Walter treats you lets me know you can have better, and if he's going to do the right thing and marry you, I don't have any complaints."

"You know Dustin had the nerve to say he already knew y'all was more than just friends," Trevor blurted as he bopped back into the room.

Bree took London, who'd started rubbing his eyes. "He's had a long day. He hung out with Walter's parents earlier today."

Timothy gave me a nod and rubbed London's back before he disappeared into another room. I guess that could have gone worse. I followed suit with a cordial nod of my own toward her family. It would take a hell of a lot more than a somewhat civil conversation for me to warm up to them. I simply needed them to know Brielle was taken care of with me.

"Need me to kick Lance's ass for you?" Trevor asked, sounding more like he was in his twenties when he was older than Bree and me.

She rolled her eyes. "That would have been helpful a few months ago."

"I'll see you later, Mama," Bree called over her shoulder as we made our way to my car.

I watched as she strapped a sleeping London into his car seat. I made a mental note to buy another one. There was no need for her to move it from my car to hers when we could both have one.

"What?" she asked from the passenger side of my car.

"Are you happy?"

"With them? My expectations are beyond low when it comes to the Barnes' family," she said dismissively.

Just as she was about to get into the car, I asked, "With me. Are you happy with me?"

"You know I am. My Mr. Right has been under my nose this

whole time," she said with a cute little giggle.

"Marry me."

She froze. "Don't say that." Bree peeked in on London, who was fast asleep in the back seat, then made her way to the driver's side where I stood. "I know how you feel about getting married."

"I changed my mind," I said, returning her smirk.

"I'm serious, Walter. After everything I've been through, you're more important."

"And after falling for you and London, I changed my mind." I pulled her against me, needing to put my hands on her. I'd wanted to touch Brielle all day.

"How is this going to work? I can't imagine you buying a ring and wearing a suit," she teased.

"I'm not doing either of those."

She twisted her head to the side in her usual, sassy manner with her eyes bucked as if to say, 'boy, what?'.

"I want you to have my grandmother's ring."

Brielle's lips parted.

"My namesake was the smartest, coolest man I've ever met, and he loved my grandmother more than he loved me. Trust me, that's saying a lot."

Bree stepped back and jumped up and down, clapping.

"Is that a yes?" I asked with a lump in my throat. The weather was still cool, but my palms were sweaty as I awaited Brielle's response.

She stuck her hand out with her palm facing up.

I slapped it like she wanted a five.

"Where is it, Walter?" she demanded.

"It's at my house. Come home with me."

Brielle's breath caught as I pulled her in for a sensual kiss. "Is a hall pass supposed to last this long?" she whispered.

"Shit, it is for us, baby."

epilogue

Bree

LONDON AND I OFFICIALLY MOVED IN WITH WALTER TWO months ago. The night my parents confronted us over the Zanaé commercial, I had him drive me home to pack a suitcase of everything we needed, knowing the rest could be packed later. It was a good thing we did.

"Baby, come look at this," I shouted to Walter.

"London, OK?" he asked with a towel wrapped around his wide frame.

I blinked rapidly, still stunned at how I'd been able to coexist as best friends with a man this fine for so long when I could barely be in the same house with him without leaking these days.

"You called me in here to get me dirty again?" he asked, matching my energy.

"Yeah, uh, no. Look." I pointed at the television where police were gathered in my old neighborhood.

His head flew in my direction as recognition washed over his handsome features. "That's buddy who waved at you, the one I didn't recognize?"

I nodded. "He was a squatter and had been hiding in the neighborhood for weeks. They just arrested him for his suspected involvement in a double homicide."

He sat down with a ghosted look on his face. "He looked shady, and I was positive I'd never seen him before." His chest heaved as he stared off at nothing.

I leaned over and kissed him on his cheek, then the corner of his mouth. His body relaxed under my touch.

"It's OK. London and I are fine," I pressed.

He stood with his fists balled. "I almost dropped the ball. I don't know what I would've done if something happened to y'all."

"We're fine, Dizzy. I've never felt safer," I said, tugging on his towel.

"We gotta get ready for work," he tried with his eyes closed in satisfaction.

"Fuck that job," I teased. "You want me home with London anyway."

"I sure as hell do, but you're just trying to make me feel better."

"Is it working?" I asked as I gripped his stiff manhood.

"Hell yeah."

I'd barely gotten Walter in my mouth when my phone rang with Lance's ringtone. He had London. Walter stilled and begrudgingly allowed me to slip from his mouth with a groan.

So far, he and Lance had been cordial with handoffs despite Walter's disappointment that I didn't follow through on Nathaniel Brown's offer to assist me with a personal injury lawsuit. It wouldn't bring me any closure to penalize Lance's stupidity. I had Walter. I already won.

I still couldn't bring myself to call Lance by his government name. He'd forever be Lance, my child's father who thought he could get away with his criminal record of cashing fraudulent checks just because he created a new identity. His last job flagged his documents, and he hadn't bothered coming clean or trying to get work since.

It helped that he and Emma were still seeing each other. She had no issues financially supporting him. It would take some time before I was ready for her to be around my son, and luckily, Lance agreed. He didn't object to Walter being around London because Dizzy had been in London's life from the beginning.

"I'm sorry," I whispered to Walt as he hurried from the room. "Hey," I said as I accepted the call on speaker phone, unable to hide my irritation.

"Hey, yourself," Lance returned in an unfamiliar tone. Walter's slides thumped against his hardwood floor, and he was back at my side with his towel refastened in no time.

"Everything good?" Walter asked, making his presence known.

I rolled my eyes at him while he shrugged unapologetically.

"Yep. London wants to see his mama. Y'all decent?"

"Yes," I said with a blush.

"Kind of," Walter muttered.

The video call rang, and I accepted right away. Lance aimed the phone at London whose heavy cheeks lifted, causing his eyes to practically disappear. "Mama. Hiiii, Mama."

My heart smiled. London needed his daddy, but it didn't make being away from him any easier. These calls did, though, and for that, I was eternally grateful.

"London Bridges," Walter crooned.

"Waaw Waa down," London sang.

Our eyes lit up as he sang the London Bridges song Walter taught him and clapped. "I miss you, buddy," Walter added.

London waved and said, "Bye, Mama."

"I guess he's over it," I added. "Thank you for letting him see me."

"Anytime," was Lance's response.

Walter pushed his bare chest back into the frame. "We appreciate it," he boomed.

Lance gave him a nod and ended the call.

"Was that necessary?"

"Yes. I told you he would love nothing more than to swipe you back from me."

"Why would I want him when I'm about to marry my best friend?"

I lifted my hand and admired my two-carat oval shaped, antique ring that originally belonged to Walter's grandmother. His grandfather loved her real big.

"You act like you love that more than you love me," Dizzy said with a frown on his face.

"Oh, speaking of my ring. I posted it on social media, and Zanaé liked and reshared it with the caption *inspiration for my new single.*"

Walter whipped out his phone and navigated to the platform heading straight for the comments.

"What are you doing?"

"Making sure nobody thirsty is commenting on your page."

I admired his profile while he scrolled through the comments, not once acknowledging Zanaé. I was so blessed to be with this handsome, crazy, territorial man.

Walter

WHEN I TOLD Bree I wasn't wearing a suit, I had no idea we'd end up having an intimate yet lavish ceremony at the *Carnelian* where it all began. Zanaé pulled out all the stops, flying and hosting everyone we wanted. She went so far as to personally greet our parents along with Chanté, Chase, and Hakeem, who were also here to enjoy their third vacation of the year and to keep an eye on London, of course.

Mason and I had grown closer as of late, but he almost shed a tear when Zanaé kissed him on the cheek. He thanked me incessantly, saying how I'd given him the best gift. It was left up for interpretation whether he was grateful for his new daughter-in-law and grandson or for his moment with Zanaé.

My mom, on the other hand, wasn't too happy about Zanaé's proximity to him. She muttered something about a young hussy. Maybe she still had feelings for my old man. Bree's father pretended to be disinterested in Zanaé because she was unsurprisingly dressed in barely there clothing like every other popstar.

We were all fans of hers, but Zanaé swooned over London. She held him as much as she could, and when she asked if she could post a picture of him, I immediately stepped in.

"We love you and we're thankful for all you've done, but I can't let you post little man on the internet. I'd get locked up hunting down trolls and pedos," I asserted.

She immediately spun on her heels to face Bree. "Girl, you won!"

"I did, didn't I," she said with her Nutella-colored eyes locked on mine.

I PACED the floor of my suite until Bree knocked on the door. I unlocked it for her, furious she wasn't staying with me for the night.

"It's tradition," she cooed.

The even glare I threw her way brought an even bigger smile to her face.

"Since when have you known me to give a damn about tradition?"

"It'll make the sex better."

"Let you tell it." I rolled my eyes, still unable to calm myself when the reality sank in that she was staying in the room next to me.

"London is going to be with Chanté and Chase for the next few days while we honeymoon, so I wanted to spend as much time with him as I can."

"London goes to sleep at eight thirty," I spat. "And he sleeps in his own bed away from your loud ass."

Bree pursed her lips and crossed her arms, wearing one of my T-shirts. There was a ninety percent chance she was naked underneath. *Damn!*

"What you over there doing?"

"I was trying to finish reading *A Naughty Rendezvous* but got interrupted by your heavy footsteps. Jada is getting confronted—about the affair—at dinner with her man. I've got to figure out how this can all be ironed out in a few pages, then I can finally get the Brown Baddies off my back about it."

"For months, you and London have been part of my nighttime routine." I pouted, not giving a shit about her smutty book.

She stepped into my adjoined room, showcasing her thick thighs when she did. My mouth watered.

"Where's the monitor?" I asked, thirsty for her proximity.

"I'm not staying. I want to be well-rested for tomorrow."

"Me too," I whined. Brielle swore that after we made love, I released my energy inside of her and therefore went straight to sleep while she took in every emotion I carried. If I was anxious or excited, for hours, she would be awake, carrying that emotion. It was the cause for many cranky morning afters on her part because I would wake up refreshed while she needed much more time to recover.

She leaned up on her toes and gave me a kiss. "I love you."

"I love you too." As soon as she turned to leave, I clapped both of her cheeks.

"Tomorrow," she fussed.

I WOKE UP IN A MOOD. Grouchy Walter was alive and well, and my mother hadn't hesitated to point it out.

"He had to sleep without his woman," Mason commented, taunting me.

Despite my irritation, I could appreciate the delicate, Bohemian Macrame wedding arch that faced the ocean opposite the bamboo chairs with the white cushions for our guests. The maxi dresses and khaki shorts our people wore were a nice touch.

The wedding planner was sugary sweet and extra patient with me. It was as though she'd been notified of my trepidation with marriage in general. She told me where to stand once our limited guests were in their seats. The ocean waves calmed me while I waited for my lady. The moment I saw her walking toward me, any doubt that I had about whether marrying her was the right thing to do left me.

She wore a silk white dress that crossed around her neck, exposing her sexy shoulders, with a high leg split that showcased her right thigh with each step she took. A train that connected to the back of her neck floated in the air with the breeze, taking my breath away.

Bree said the only part of the ceremony she wanted to keep was exchanging vows. Her father was the only one who was adamantly against us not using an ordained minister during the ceremony. Bree convinced him to let it go when she asked him to be our officiant. He was so honored he didn't seem to mind it would be on paper only.

When she was finally in front of me, my eyes watered. I was so overcome with emotion that she leaned over and wiped a tear from my eye.

"I love you," I whispered.

"I know," was her sassy response.

She shifted her body toward our loved ones: my parents, her parents, Chanté, and Chase, who sat with Hakeem and London, and Zanaé and her man, Rod.

"Thank y'all for being here to support our very non-traditional ceremony."

She turned back toward me, and my heart literally skipped a beat.

"I feel like I've known you for two lifetimes. You were my best friend, my hall pass, and now my husband."

"Did she say hall pass?" Timothy asked loudly.

Chanté choked on her spit, laughing.

"I carry you in my heart, no matter where you are. I want nothing but the best for you, even if that meant I would never become a Simmons."

"Say it again," I said.

"Say what?" She blushed.

"That you're a Simmons."

"I'm a Simmons."

"I know that's right," Chanté and Zanaé said in unison, high fiving each other when they did.

"This ain't a wedding," Timothy complained.

"Leave these kids alone. This is how they want it. Can you blame them after the stunt London's father pulled?" Erica fussed.

I was grateful she hadn't said his name, especially on a day like today.

"I'm sorry, baby. Continue," I said with a wink, satisfied that she was turned on. It was obvious to me in the way she shifted under my gaze.

"I was willing to pass on being married just to continue what we have, but you said you saw marriage differently." She sniffed, and my throat tightened. Her love for me had grown to a level I never thought was possible.

"I love you, Walter, from now until forever."

She leaned up and kissed me gently.

I cleared my throat and steadied myself to express my love for my lady in words.

"I never thought I'd find the love the original Walter Simmons, my grandfather and namesake, spoke of. He was my best friend and ally in this world until I met you. I was a child when he talked about how much he loved my grandmother. Grandpa Simmons said he'd get a funny feeling every time my grandmother entered a room. I asked him if maybe he was allergic to her perfume."

Everyone burst into laughter at my youthful mindset.

"Then I got older, and I dismissed my grandfather's butterflies as lust. I got a similar reaction when I saw a beautiful woman too. The realities of this racist world and the unfair systems we currently live in completely turned me off to the idea of marriage. I couldn't understand why my favorite people in the world," I paused as my eyes landed on my mother then back on Bree, "would allow themselves to be treated less than what they deserved in the name of marriage."

Tears streamed down my mother's face, and I didn't miss how she let my father wrap his arm around her shoulder. Identical tears adorned Brielle's face, and a wave of anger flowed through me at the way her trifling ex handled her.

I steadied my breath and continued. "You changed my mind, which is not an easy thing to do."

She nodded her head in agreement.

Commotion at my left distracted Bree and me when London squirmed in Chanté's arms. Bree was willing to ignore it for the sake of the ceremony, although it killed her not to go to him. He was a good baby, but seeing his mama and me this close was torture since he couldn't get to us.

"Hold up a sec," I told them and took long strides in his direction, unbothered that the ceremony would have to wait.

"Come here, London Bridges," I said as he stretched his arms up. He was more handsome than ever in his white dress shirt and beige khaki shorts with matching suspenders and bow tie.

There were coos and ahhs for the handsome guy as I rejoined his mother. He waved and said "Hi, Mama."

"Hi, baby."

"Where was I?"

"I changed your mind," my wife said with a smirk on her face. My heart skipped a beat with the new endearment because no one could take it away from me that legally, and in all the other ways that mattered, I was Brielle's first husband.

"Right. You changed my outlook on marriage because you are the only woman I've met willing to sacrifice a ring for me. I already told you I'd walk through hell with gasoline drawers on. I'm in it to win it, Bree."

"Mercy," her mother spat at my use of the word hell.

I leaned in and kissed my woman, then whispered in her ear. "When London goes to sleep, can I record us?" I found her eyes and was floored when I saw her fiery, steady gaze.

"I'm yours, Walter. You can do whatever you want to me."

THE END

in real life...

I write black love stories because I am an advocate for healthy love between black men and women. I seek to empower women to create the energy from my fictitious books in their real lives. After each of my titles, I'm going to feature real love stories. My second couple is Jonathan and Tiffany.

1. *Tiffany*, **how did you meet?**

On the online dating app, Tagged. My best friend convinced me to create an account for 2 weeks. A couple of days before I planned to delete my account, he sent me a message, saying "Hey beautiful"

1. *Jonathan*, **what is your favorite quality about your partner?**

Definitely her energy. Her energy brings out the best in everyone she is around. Her presence comforts me and brightens my day.

1. *Tiffany,* **what is your pet peeve about your partner? (The thing that drives you nuts about them, but they are worth looking past it)**

He loves to affectionately pinch my nose. I give him the side eye every time he does it

1. *Jonathan and Tiffany,* what is your advice for people currently looking for love?

1) Don't limit yourself to your usual "type."

2) Heal past heartbreaks/traumas so that your heart is truly open to receiving love.

3) Have fun in the dating stage! Every date will tell you more about what you want and don't want.

afterword

Thank you for finishing *A Justified Hall Pass*.

If you enjoyed this story, **leave me a five-star rating and review on Amazon, and a positive review on Goodreads** and **TikTok.** And recommend it to your friends.

Also, I share freebies, sneak peeks, and discounts for sensual products on my mailing and SMS list! Sign up here.

Mailing list

Get steamy texts from your favorite book baes 💋

Thank you in advance,

Denise Essex

also by denise essex

One of the best ways to support me as an indie author is to purchase my paperbacks. Find them on Amazon, or for a signed copy, visit my Etsy store.

More *Sweet Heat* eBook Reads below 💋

Cindy Ella

My Book

Daddy's Maybe

My Book

Prison Bae

https://bit.ly/PrisonBaeTrey

The Firemen's Ball: A Masquerade Affair

My Book

The Pleasure Package

https://bit.ly/pleasurepackage

A Naughty Rendezvous

https://bit.ly/ANaughtyRendezvous

Love in the same strip club

https://bit.ly/SameStripClub

Heat Haven Heaux-Tell: Three Novellas

https://bit.ly/HeatHaven

The College Route

https://bit.ly/TheCollegeRoute

I Found Her

https://amzn.to/3VmWLm7

The Visiting Professor

https://bit.ly/TheVisitingProfessor

Gone For a Soldier

https://bit.ly/GoneForASoldier

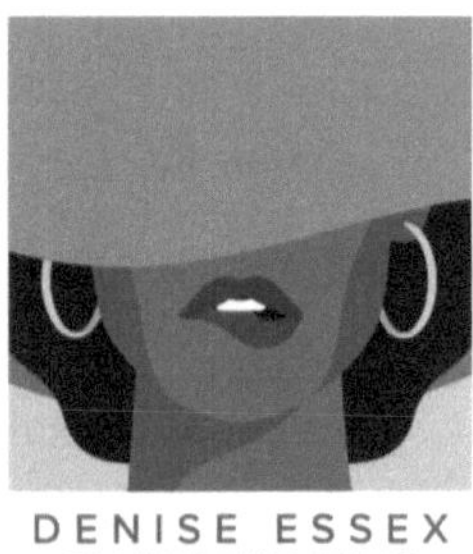

Where to find me in these intanet streets 💋

TikTok: tiktok.com/@deniseessex222 **(Help me reach 2K 🎉)**

Amazon Author Page: https://www.amazon.com/author/denise_essex

Readers Group: https://www.face-book.com/groups/deniseessexheatseekers

Facebook page: https://www.facebook.com/DeniseEssexAuthor

INSTAGRAM: https://www.instagram.com/deniseessex222/

IG Handle: @DeniseEssex222

TikTok: @DeniseEssex222

Twitter: @DeniseEssex222